Remains
to be
Seen

Remains
to be
Seen

Elizabeth
Cadell

WILLIAM MORROW AND COMPANY, INC.

New York 1983

Library of Congress Catalog Card Number: 83-61741

ISBN: 0-688-02177-8

Printed in the United States of America

First U.S. Edition

1 2 3 4 5 6 7 8 9 10

1

This being a midweek afternoon, Victoria station was not crowded. The suburban shoppers had gone home, the rush hour had not begun; there were no porters in sight, and few travellers, so that Philippa Lyle, on her way to board the train to Canterbury, felt reasonably certain that she would be able to get a compartment to herself. She looked forward to putting her feet up, snatching some sleep and recovering the sense of time disorganised by her transatlantic flight.

These pleasant anticipations were dispelled by the sight of two familiar and far from welcome figures—an elderly man and woman—who were handing in their tickets at the barrier. They were Mr. and Mrs. Beetham, neighbours who had known her since she was born and who since that time had busied themselves, unasked, in her affairs.

There was no hope of evading them. She was in full view and they had only to glance behind them—but there was a faint hope that they would board the train without a backward look. This Mrs. Beetham did, but

5

her husband, on the point of following her into the compartment, paused to glance along the platform. He saw Philippa, and a word to his wife brought her to the window. Together they waited for her to draw near, and then Mrs. Beetham's loud, chairman-of-committee voice hailed her.

"Hello there, Philippa. I said—didn't I say, Harold?— that you might possibly be travelling down on this train. Come in here. Harold will see that nobody else gets in." She loosened her lightweight coat, took a corner seat and strewed a number of small packages on to the vacant places. "Is that all the luggage you've brought?"

"Yes." Philippa swung two suitcases onto the rack, sat down and resigned herself to a journey during which Mrs. Beetham would talk nonstop until they reached Canterbury. There was nothing to be done but give monosyllabic answers to impertinent questions and make certain that she would not be trapped into travelling with them on the last stage of the journey—twenty miles by bus to the small town of Montoak.

"Nice suitcases. You bought them in Canada, I suppose?" Mrs. Beetham enquired.

"Yes."

"Of course, you won't need much luggage for the month you're going to be in England. It is a month, isn't it?"

"Two."

Mrs. Beetham had opened a capacious handbag and taken out powder compact and lipstick. As she applied them, Philippa looked at her and thought that the passing years seemed to make no difference to her appearance. Thin, tall, smartly dressed, copper-tinted wig. Judging her by the light of two years' absence, Philippa decided that in her long-past youth she must have been attractive, so it was difficult to understand why she had married Mr. Beetham, who even in youth

6

must have been fat and florid and of a surly disposition. His lips were a thin, grim line and he seldom opened them except to supplement his wife's comments on the general disagreeableness of the world. Philippa thought it inexplicable that with good health, a comfortable income and few domestic problems, they saw nothing in life to be in the least thankful for.

The whistle blew, train doors were banged. Mrs. Beetham put away her make-up, Mr. Beetham stepped into the compartment and sat opposite his wife. The train moved smoothly out into the late May sunshine; the questions were resumed.

"It's a pity your mother couldn't come to London to meet you. I went in to see her yesterday—she's better, but the doctor said that after flu, she ought to be careful. I haven't congratulated you on your engagement. I suppose you'll be married as soon as you get back to Canada?"

"Yes."

"Such a pity your mother won't meet your fiancé."

"She will."

"Oh? You don't mean she's actually going over . . . "

"No. He's coming to England."

"For how long?"

"Two weeks."

"I suppose you'll go back together?"

"Yes."

"I was glad to hear that he's quite well off. Your mother had to make a great many sacrifices after your father left her."

Philippa did not trouble to point out that her mother had had to make no sacrifices, and that her husband had left her only because she refused to accompany him to Canada.

"I suppose it was useless to try and persuade your mother to go over for the wedding?"

7

"Yes."

Silly question, she thought, since Mrs. Beetham and all the other residents of the estate known as the Ridge at Montoak knew that her mother seldom left home—a reaction against the years during which she had trailed after a footloose father, and then after an even more peripatetic husband. Her mother would not willingly undertake a journey to Canterbury, much less travel all the way to Canada.

They were leaving houses and streets behind; Philippa looked out at the green fields with the grazing cows, the trees in spring dress, the pale blue English sky. It looked like a postcard view, a pocket sized country. But with every curve of the line, she felt more at home; it was almost as though she had never left.

"How," Mrs. Beetham wanted to know, "did you get on with your father?"

"Very well."

"Of course you must have remembered him quite well. You were eight when he left."

"Nine," corrected Mr. Beetham.

"Nine. Did you like his wife?"

"Yes." And no, she added to herself.

"I'm sure you would rather have been married in England. Would it have been so difficult to arrange?"

Patiently, Philippa explained that her fiancé's grandfather—his only near relative—was old and infirm and had been forbidden by his doctor to undertake the journey to England.

She leaned back and closed her eyes—a hint that Mrs. Beetham had never been known to take. A change in the direction of the train brought a shaft of sunlight on to Philippa's hair, turning it to gold, and Mr. Beetham, from his corner, told himself grudgingly that she had grown into a good-looking young woman. Extraordinary. At fifteen, she had been a scruffy teenager

8

with a plain, flat face, cycling dangerously down the slope past his house in company with the other children who lived on the Ridge, all yelling, all wild and all in need of discipline. And look at her now: quiet, self possessed, a near beauty. He didn't think much of the modern way of dressing. Too casual. None of the neatness, none of the elegance women had had when he was a young man.

She opened her eyes, roused by the fact that the questions had ceased and Mrs. Beetham was actually saying something interesting.

" . . . don't know how much you've been able to gather from your mother's letters about what's been going on at Montoak since you went away."

"Well, she's been keeping me in touch with all the . . . "

"I'm not a vindictive woman, I hope, but that's what I feel—vindictive—every time I think of that young man, Ward Rowallen. He's been the cause of it all. He pestered the authorities, he brought down so-called experts, he ignored every protest made by those of us living on the Ridge—we were, after all, the ones who were to be affected. When he went so far as to have that aerial survey made . . . after that there was no hope of stopping the thing. I don't want to claim that I've suffered more than anybody else, but when you see our beautiful house surrounded by workmen and trucks and—you know, I can hardly believe it yet—a car park. A hideous car park, immediately next door to us, below our very windows. Busloads of sightseers and tourists, noise, petrol fumes . . . well, you'll see. When all this began, when they gave the Plesseys notice, I felt thankful that our house was at least our own; they couldn't turn us out. But now I'm not so sure. We've had enough and we're beginning to think about moving, selling up and going to live somewhere else. We went to see the house agents in Canterbury last week, and we found—as we expected, of course—that we can't ask a quarter of what it cost us to build. And no hope of any kind of compensation."

"Are the Plesseys still . . . "

" . . . in their house? Yes. Didn't your mother tell you?"

"She hasn't mentioned them lately."

"They were given a year's notice. They've been offered alternative accommodation, but none of it was of the kind they could bring themselves to accept. Nothing that they could possibly live in, after all those years in their house on the Ridge which they had made so comfortable. It was a pity they decided to rent. They should have bought—as Harold and I did, as your father did, as Mr. Luton and the Armitages did. But, of course, the Plesseys hadn't the money to buy—disgraceful, when you think of their mother living in luxury and not allowing them a penny. The saddest part for them now is having to leave that lovely Japanese garden that they've made with such patience and labour. Who will look after it when they've gone?"

"Who . . . " began Philippa.

"The ironic part of all this is that if we'd thought seriously about it years ago, we could have bought the land that they've built the car park on. The Plesseys never wanted all their ground. The part beyond the Japanese gardens was too much for them to cultivate, and they couldn't afford a gardener. For a time Harold and I thought of making an offer for it, but we had more than enough land as it was, so Harold merely offered to plant shrubs on it—which he did. If only we could have foreseen that one day there would be a car park . . . "

"Who will have the house when the Plesseys go?"

"Nobody. It's to be used for what they call

10

administrative offices. That will show you how much this affair has mushroomed in the two years you've been away. Administrative offices! Clerks and typists and printed leaflets of information about the excavations. Why couldn't they have left the Plesseys where they were, and used that other leasehold house—the Springers'—for Administrative offices? At least that would have rid us of the Springer family. It's a pity that people of that kind ever came to the Ridge. But what does it matter, today? The whole estate is ruined.''

She stopped to take breath and her husband filled in the pause with a corroborative growl.

''Ruined.''

''Your mother, I'm sorry to say, has from the very beginning been on the side of the despoilers. It was all very well for her to follow the experts round the site and attend lectures on the Roman occupation—she hadn't to endure the noise and the dust and the devastation that was going on round our house. She—Harold, the train's stopping. Don't let anybody in.''

Her husband took up his stand in the doorway, assuming an expression so forbidding that nobody made any attempt to enter.

Philippa waited with some impatience for the train to move again. It was the first time she remembered feeling any desire to hear Mrs. Beetham's voice—but she was beginning to realise that her mother's letters, regular and informative though they had been, had conveyed little of the effect that the last two years had had on the residents of the Ridge. She had given all the facts: the chance discovery, by Ward Rowallen, of a fragment of Roman pottery, his subsequent determination to follow up the find and see where the investigations led; the aerial survey and the sensational discovery of remains buried beneath the central basin of the Ridge. But she

11

had not described the distress of Laura and Selma Plessey, who not only had to leave the house in which they had lived for the past twenty-four years, but who would have to abandon the Japanese garden which had become a kind of local showpiece and to which, under strict supervision, the children living on the Ridge had sometimes had access. She had not conveyed Mrs. Beetham's sense of outrage at the invasion of the once peaceful Ridge by tourists and sightseers.

The train went on. Mrs. Beetham went on.

"Two years. Two years of clearing, of destroying that lovely little park and its bushes and flower gardens. To say nothing of the children's playground. We opened our newspapers one morning to find Montoak in the headlines. And four entire pages in the *Illustrated London News*. Don't run away with the idea that the changes were only taking place on the Ridge. No. By no means. The town . . . It was a dull little town and it took some time to wake up to what was going on, but when it did? Money. There was money to be made. Every house with a spare bedroom offered bed and breakfast to the students working on the site. Every café, every boarding house began to offer what was presumed to be the kind of food the visiting foreigners wanted—hamburgers for the Americans, curry messes for the Indians and Pakistanis, heaven knows what for the West Indians. Grocers and butchers are now prepared to instruct you on the probable date of the discoveries. Schoolgirls regale you with facts about Claudius and Aulus Plautius and Agricola. I expect any moment to see togas for sale in the shop windows," she ended bitterly.

"My mother said that people had protested . . . "

"Oh, protested! At the beginning, yes. When it was known that the park was to be dug up, people protested—but how many people ever used that park? A handful. Parents protested when the children's

12

playground was demolished—but again, there weren't enough of them to make any impact. And once the tourists began to arrive, and the busloads of sightseers, nobody thought of anything but profit. Montoak is on the map. You can comfort yourself with that reflection when you look out of your windows and see stones and pillars instead of grass and flowers."

"My mother said they'd just discovered . . . "

" . . . part of a Roman pavement. Yes. On the very edge of the Plessey house. So there'll be more digging. Where, where is it going to end?" Her voice, already high with anger, became shrill. "None of it makes sense to me. We all know that the Romans invaded and occupied Britain. We all know that they built villas and baths and roads and walls. I daresay this train is at this very moment going over buried baths—are we to dig up the whole of our lovely countryside in order to uncover more and more sites? Anyone who's interested can drive to the sites that have already been excavated. Are we to destroy the beauties of today to dig up the Roman past?"

She paused, but neither Philippa nor Mr. Beetham had an answer.

"I can talk to you like this," she went on more calmly, "but if I uttered one word of it in the town, I'd be pointed out as uneducated, uncooperative and un-civic-minded. So I say nothing."

The train drew up beside a platform on which there were so many waiting passengers that it was useless for Harold to stand guard. A mother and two small children entered, and Mrs. Beetham, snatching her packages out of harm's way, sat in moody silence, while her husband opened his newspaper and disappeared behind it. Philippa, after waiting in vain for the mother to quell the two restive children, took out pad and pencil and drew animal sketches that kept them interested and amused. As she absently sketched ponies and mice, she let her mind rest on the changes that Mrs. Beetham had so bitterly described.

The Ridge . . .

It had been, thirty years earlier, a large area of waste land belonging to the only family of note in the district: a line of baronets named Rowallen who owned an ancient manor house on the low hill which formed a barrier between the town of Montoak and the farmlands bordering the sea. The family had long been impoverished, and successive generations had sold most of what once had been vast properties. The Ridge was the last remaining land in their possession; they offered it for sale and it was bought by the town authorities. It was a kind of very large, shallow basin, the flat, central area of which was scheduled to be a park and a children's playground, while the higher surrounding part was to be divided into sites varying from two to six acres, and sold for building. The sides of the basin sloped down from the Manor hill in the form of two embracing arms—a horseshoe whose open end was eventually filled by the park gates. One of the arms was named North Ridge, the other South Ridge. Where the arms reached the level of the gates, the authorities built two small houses which they offered on twenty-five-year leases.

The Beethams were the first to settle on the Ridge. Archsnobs, they hoped that the high prices asked would keep out what they called undesirable elements. This hope brightened when the leasehold house next door to them was taken by two unmarried sisters named Plessey, both Honourables. After this satisfactory beginning, however, the level of society fell slightly. The site on the other side of the Beethams was bought by an accountant named Armitage, with his wife and small son. On the opposite side of the Ridge, the highest site was bought by a couple named Lyle, the man a portrait painter of whom the Beethams had never heard. Next door to them came an architect named Luton, with his wife. There only remained the leasehold house on the other side of the gates, and this, to the chagrin of the Beethams, was rented by a builder from London, a cockney who had made his fortune and was on the point of retirement. With him came his stout and easy-going wife, and four small children.

The houses varied greatly in size and design, but all had been built at a time when resident servants were difficult to find, and so were planned on labour-saving lines. There were large windows, easy-to-clean floors, modern kitchens and heating, and modern domestic equipment.

Of the old baronet on the hill nobody saw more than occasional glimpses. He was a widower; he had been twice married, but the first marriage had been childless. The second, to a young Swedish woman, had produced a son, Edward, known as Ward who, until his mother's death, had spent most of his vacations with her relations in Sweden. Only when he had succeeded to the title at the age of fifteen did he give any sign of considering the Manor as his home.

The park and the children's playground had been completed just before Philippa was born. She tried to imagine the Ridge without its central carpet of colour—flowering shrubs, flowerbeds, smooth green grass. It was impossible to visualise a car park next to the Beethams' house, a dignified mansion with two circular towers and curving balconies. It was impossible to think of the Ridge without the Plesseys, who spent all their spare time beautifying their Japanese garden.

The train reached Canterbury. Mr. Beetham lifted

down Philippa's suitcases. Mrs. Beetham collected packages.

"I'm sorry we can't offer you a lift," she told Philippa, "Harold has some business to do in Canterbury."

"That's all right. I'll get a bus," Philippa said.

"Tell your mother I'll look in and see her soon."

Philippa left them as soon as she had got through the barrier. She walked into the road and went across to the bus station. As she did so, she heard her name called. Turning, she found coming towards her Denise Luton—like herself, born on the Ridge—a next-door neighbour and lifelong companion.

She was a year older than Philippa. They had attended the same kindergarten in Montoak and the same co-educational school in Canterbury. Denise's home life had not been happy: her father—an architect who referred to himself as retired, but who accepted most of the commissions that came his way—was a man dedicated to his own comfort, and the house revolved round his whims. His wife was unable to oppose him, since the first signs of contradiction or confrontation produced in her husband symptoms too alarming to have been entirely assumed. Against this background Denise had grown up, resigned all her life to giving up any plan, however cherished, that might displease her father and bring on one of his heart attacks.

Perhaps this cloud over her childhood accounted for her lack of success at school. Intelligent and hard working, she had never achieved the first place in class. Good at games, she had never played in the first team. A swift runner, she had never succeeded in breasting the tape ahead of her rivals.

Her mother died when she was in her last year at school. Denise was hoping to go on to university, but this plan caused Mr. Luton a series of such severe attacks that it was decided that she would take a part time job in Montoak and spend the rest of her time looking after her father. When, three years later, he unexpectedly and unwisely remarried, she looked forward to sharing her duties with her stepmother. The new Mrs. Luton, however, was not a woman who was interested in family life. Relations between them grew so strained that at last Denise decided to leave home. It was a foolish decision; the house had been left to her by her mother, and she was warned that if she left it she would find it very difficult to get it away from her father and his new wife. Nothing, however, could stop her; she announced her decision of taking rooms near her job in Montoak. She had been eighteen. Now she was twenty-three, and was bitterly regretting having left.

"Why aren't you at work?" Philippa asked her.

"I told the boss my grandmother was dying, and came to meet you." She took one of the suitcases. "Nice to have you back."

"How did you know I'd be on this train?"

"Your mother rang London airport and they said your plane would be on time. I worked it out from there. I brought your car—you can drive me back to the Springers. It's in the car park."

"Let's go."

"I passed the Beethams," Denise said as they went. "Did you see them on the train?"

"I was trapped in the same compartment."

"My God, what a journey! I bet she told you what she's been suffering."

"I got a clearer idea of what's been going on than I did from all your or my mother's letters. You told me about the digging, so did she, but I hadn't got a picture of what the digging had done to the town—and to the Ridge."

"Never mind the Ridge for the moment." Denise

opened the back of the car, disposed of the suitcase and took her place beside Philippa. "Drive slowly—there's so much to talk about."

"Such as Reid, for example? How is he?"

"Never mind Reid, either. First tell me about this man you've decided to marry."

"I told you."

"Why was it so sudden? You're sure you know what you're doing?"

"Of course I know."

"It shook me, the news that you were going to marry a Canadian and stay over there for the rest of your life. I'd always thought that you were a part of this place—The Ridge. You and I, both. Born here, brought up here, all our . . . our associations here. I suppose I was silly to take it for granted that we'd both marry and settle down here."

"It wasn't silly. I thought so, too, when I left here two years ago."

"What's the attraction, exactly? The man, of course—but what else? The—what would you call it!—the way of life over there?"

Philippa hesitated. She had not asked herself many questions when she had agreed to marry Dudley Errol. She had denied Denise's statement of suddenness, but she knew that there had been a time, at the beginning of her engagement, when she had had the feeling of having dived into deep waters and of difficulty in finding her way to the surface. She had realised since then that she had, in a sense, surrendered to circumstances. Dudley Errol had been regarded as a matrimonial prize, and nobody had expected her to reject him. His method of pursuit had been to persuade her to join him on his expeditions—sailing, swimming, wind-surfing, skiing. He was an expert in most athletic fields, and she had enjoyed the effort of keeping up with him.

18

Almost all their time together had been passed in outdoor activities. She had admired his prowess, but he had put little or no pressure on her to make love. Her eventual agreement to marry him had come about through the pleasure she found in his company, the absence of any urgent demands and, above all, the sense of security she enjoyed because of his reliability, his solidity and his unfailing protectiveness. It was the assurance of these qualities that had helped her in such moments of doubt. Where, she had asked herself, could she find a better husband? The answer—nowhere. There had been no rivals to challenge him.

"You're dreaming," she heard Denise say. "I asked you whether it was the Canadian way of life you fell for."

"No. If I could have chosen, I'd rather have lived here. But you have to live where your husband lives."

"That's true. But it makes it easier if he's where you like to be. Do you feel like a Canadian?"

"No. Not that there's much difference in being a housewife here or there."

"How about freezing for part of the year?"

"We'll be living in Vancouver—we won't freeze."

"Has this man—Dudley—any kind of tie-up with England?"

"What do you mean by tie-ups?"

"Business associates, friends, relations?"

"No."

"I've got a feeling—maybe I shouldn't say so—that if you'd come home earlier, this business of marrying over there wouldn't have come up. What kept you there a whole two years?"

"Visiting my mother's aunts, for the first year."

"There are only four of them, aren't there? How could you string them out over a year?"

"They live hundreds of miles apart, for one thing.

19

And they expected me to stay for months—which I did.''

''Your prime purpose in going was to get to know your father.''

''I saw enough of his wife when I first got there to know that I couldn't live with them for long, and I wanted to see as much of Canada as I could. The aunts were in a way an excuse. One of them lived in Toronto—very rich, very towny. Another of them was in British Columbia, right across on the other side of the continent. She was the nicest—gorgeous garden, lovely house by the sea, full of gadgets and gimmicks. In the morning you just pressed a button and your bedroom curtains opened, and there was the Pacific outside your window. It was rather lost on me, because I always sleep . . . ''

'' . . . with your curtains open. I know. Where were the other two aunts?''

''One lived at Banff, and the other was in Saskatchewan. So you see it wasn't a case of dropping in for a weekend.''

''Well, dropping in for a weekend isn't going to be easy if you're going to settle in Vancouver. The fare will be the first obstacle. Has this Dudley got enough money for you to make frequent trips to England?''

''I'll make frequent trips.''

''Will I like him?''

''I think so. At first he might strike you as being a bit . . . well, unforthcoming. He's rather quiet. He's a good athlete—good at most games, wonderful skier, wins tennis tournaments. Now tell me about Reid.''

''Are you really in love?''

''Why would I be getting married if I weren't in love?''

''I don't know. You're odd in some ways. I think I know all about you, and then all at once you change, like writing one minute to say you were looking forward to coming home soon, and then saying no, you'd decided to marry this . . . what's his name again?''

"Dudley Errol.''

"Well, I stick to what I said—it was a bit sudden. We all thought so.''

"It wasn't. He asked me twice and I said no. The third time, I said yes.''

"I suppose I'm comparing it to the way Reid and I got together. Ours was one of those creep-up-slowly-and-catch-you affairs.''

"How's it going?''

"Deadlock.''

"You told your father you were going to marry Reid?''

"Yes. He said, Fine, Reid would find a house and we'd go and live in it. He also said that husbands provided the home—not the wives. Some husbands do. Reid's quite prepared to, but why should he? The house on the Ridge is mine. I know I walked out, but now I've got a right to go back—I'm planning to marry, and it would suit my husband and me very well to live in my house. To which he answered that Reid Springer was well able to afford a house, and he saw no reason for turning him and his wife out of theirs.''

"He called it theirs?''

"Yes. It's a hellish situation. I'm sick of people pointing out that it's legally mine. How does it being legally mine help? Can I go to law and have my father evicted and have him staging his death scene on the pavement? Can I? So we fall back on the moral right, and that's getting me nowhere.''

"What's Reid's attitude?''

"He's all for leaving them in the house, getting one of our own and getting married and settling down. It's only me that's fighting. I may be pigheaded, but I was

21

born in that house and I know people think it looks a bit too St. Tropez to fit into the Ridge, but I've always loved it and I want it. I want that ghastly woman out of it. I want to live in it with Reid. But my father isn't going to move—so, as I said, deadlock."

"Do you think . . . ?"

"Do I think what?"

"Do you think that if Reid had been anybody else, someone he approved of, he would have been more willing to . . ."

"No. Reid being who and what he is just gives my father an extra excuse for staying on. He tells people—and she tells people, imagine her damn nerve! —that refusing to get out of the house may make me reconsider, in other words, I could give up Reid and they'd pretend to be willing to let me have the house." She paused. "It's a funny thing, I know my father's got a lot of faults, but somehow I think I could have got on with him—got on to some kind of terms—if he hadn't remarried. By which I mean, of course, if he hadn't married that awful woman."

"What does Reid think of it all?"

"What does Reid ever think? He's always thought my father was wildly funny, all that dead-and-gone snobbishness, like the Beethams. And he calls my step-mother a you-know-what, and he's right. As far as he's concerned, they can go on living in the house and welcome. That's him all over: 'Let the other chap take it away, it's too hot to get into a fight.' You know Reid."

Philippa, who had seldom thought of Reid Springer during the past two years, brought him into focus. Twenty-eight, a long pole of a man with doormat hair, small humorous eyes hidden behind strong lenses, large uneven teeth and a cockney accent. Jeans and crumpled shirts. Like all his family, easygoing, untroubled by the opinion of the Beethams or Mr. Luton; son of an

22

extremely prosperous father, but preferring to make his own way in the world. To Denise, for the past six years, progressively companion, friend and lover—but she was under no illusions as to his lack of social graces.

"He's grown a moustache," she offered apologetically. "It suits him. It makes him look . . . well, not handsome, you couldn't expect that, but he looks less plain. I know he's pretty awful to the eye, but I'm no beauty myself, am I?"

No, no beauty, Philippa admitted to herself. Brown, intelligent eyes, thick unfettered hair, almost invisible nose and large mouth. No beauty—but, like Reid, honest and straightforward and outspoken. In Reid's case, too outspoken.

"Did I tell you that Reid's got four vans now?"

"Three, you said."

"Well now it's four. And orders rolling in—and money. Funny. When he had this idea of being self employed, and bought a van and started on this fetch-and-carry racket, who would have thought what a success it would be? Four vans, four drivers—his ambition is to be able to get a fleet of eight and then sit back and just send them out. Did I tell you that he wants his brother Ronnie to give up his job and drive a van? Ronnie's keen, but his wife says no, he's got a decent job, a nine-to-five one so she knows when to expect him home—instead of never knowing when he's coming or going. Sylvie's working for Reid now."

"*Sylvie*? Sylvie Springer? Driving a van?"

"No. She'd have liked to, but Reid said no because it isn't only driving, it's being able to load and unload stuff. She's running the office."

"You told me she'd gone into films."

"She's been into everything."

"Wasn't she going to get married to . . . forget his

23

name, the man who works in the same office as Ronnie?''

"She wasn't going to get married to anybody. Marriage isn't on her books, anyway not yet awhile. Did I tell you she went after Justin Armitage?''

"Yes.''

"We all told her it was a waste of time—he's never looked at a girl. I always had a feeling he might have gone after you if you'd given him any encouragement.'' She drew a deep, contented breath. "It's nice to be able to talk to you again. I missed you. I suppose you know all about the Plesseys having to move?''

"Yes.''

"Reid says they'll be the next—the Springers, I mean. They only rent, like the Plesseys, and Reid says it won't be long before they'll be given notice. He asked Ward if he knew anything, but Ward said no.''

"What's Ward got to do with it?''

Denise gave her a surprised glance.

"Ward? He knows all about everything connected with the excavations. He's got a job on the site now.''

"Ward—*working*?''

"Well, in a way. He took over from the man who was doing the cataloguing. I don't think they pay him much, if they pay him at all, so what he uses for money, I wouldn't know. He used to make ends meet by spending all his free time with his Swedish relations, but he's fixed here now. He regards the whole operation as his baby—and so it is. In the early stages everyone treated him as though he was a crank with an oversized bee in his bonnet, but when it was photographed from the air and the experts and the bigwigs started rolling in, he was the one they consulted when they needed to consult. I wish you'd been here. It took a long time for the town to wake up, but when it did there was a rush to volunteer for jobs. Old men got out of their beds and

24

turned up claiming to be classical scholars; students came in droves, teenagers tried to join the dig. And the whole lot of them got sent home. From the start, it was a completely professional affair. No amateurs admitted except under the strictest supervision. The cafés and the restaurants began to do roaring business. There's a new fleet of taxis, and extra buses laid on from Canterbury. There isn't a decent hotel, but I daresay they'll build one soon."

They were nearing the town. It was not large and it was far from picturesque. Wherever she looked, Philippa saw signs of development—a new shopping complex, two blocks of flats. She drove down the narrow High Street and then along streets lined with small uniform houses. A large new garage on the right, an almost-as-new church on the left, and then she was going up the gradual rise to the shoulder of the hill on whose summit stood the ancient manor owned by the Rowallens.

"You won't be able to see anything of the site from the road," Denise said. "The wall—the wall that used to surround the park—hides it all. But you'll pass the new car park."

Philippa had stopped the car and was looking through the natural arch of branches that gave entrance to the Ridge. From this point, the road began a gradual descent, passing the three houses built on the North Ridge—the Armitages, the Beethams and the Plesseys. At the bottom was a curve and then came the park gates and the ascent past the three houses on the South Ridge—the Springers, the Lutons and the Lyles—after which the road led back to the town.

"It's strange," Denise said meditatively, "that your going away made a kind of break between the past and the present. The past, as far as the Ridge is concerned, is dead. You left six well kept houses, a park

25

and a playground—a residential estate which was getting a bit run down but was still what the estate agents call desirable. All that's gone. All we are now is some houses surrounding a large area of Roman remains. The Plesseys are going. The Beethams say they'll go, and as I just told you, Reid says it won't be long before his family gets notice to quit.''

Philippa looked at her with a frown.

"But if they'd wanted the house, they would have . . . ''

" . . . given the Springers notice earlier? Reid says they'll need it when they realise what a lot of finds there are to put on show. If they do get notice to get out, Reid's father and mother will go back to London. Reid and I will find somewhere, and Ronnie and his wife and the children will go with the parents. Parry—well, where do international football stars live? Sylvie will do as she's done since she was seventeen—find a man to take care of her.''

Philippa spoke in a musing tone.

"It was fun," she said slowly.

"Living here? Yes, it was fun—while it lasted. I suppose being, in a way, separated from the town made the kids on the Ridge into a sort of group. Gang. Remember how Reid was always the leader? Ronnie and Parry tagged along behind him, and so did Sylvie.''

"So did I. So did you. The only one who didn't tag along was Ward.''

Ward Rowallen had always joined them when he was at home, and had given them the run of the Manor grounds, which afforded a variety of playgrounds: the glen for picnics, the pool for bathing, the paddocks for impromptu gymkhanas on a collection of shaggy ponies. At Philippa's house, in the large, unused dining room, they assembled to play records. In the Springers'

26

hospitable well stocked kitchen they had gathered round the table while Mrs. Springer, stout and smiling, served pancakes or pizzas. They held bicycle races along the three mile stretch of road that led across the farmlands and ended at a small, stony beach. In winter they tobogganed down the slopes from the Manor, or down the roads of North or South Ridge. And then they grew up, and Mr. Luton wakened too late to the fact that his daughter was seeing too much of Reid Springer, and the talent scouts recognised Reid's younger brother Parry's potential as a footballer and removed him to a life of training and teams and transfers; and his elder brother, Ronnie, married a neighbouring farmer's daughter and settled with her into a mobile home on his father-in-law's land; until his sister Sylvie went to London to make her fortune and found it easier to spend someone else's; and Philippa and Denise got jobs and Justin went to work in his father's accountancy office in Mont-oak . . .

"Seems an awfully long time ago," remarked Denise.

"Yes, it does."

Philippa put the car into gear and drove slowly down the slope. The first sign of change came when they had passed the Armitage house. The entrance to the house next door—the Beethams'—was as she remembered it, but beyond it, the area the Plesseys had not wanted to use and on which Mr. Beetham had planted flowering shrubs, was now a large car park. It was well designed and well kept, but it was—as Mrs. Beetham had lamented—directly below their windows.

"You're lucky—you can't see it from your house," Denise said. "Your windows look down on to the Roman remains."

Philippa was driving round the curve at the bottom of the slope. She passed the park gates, the open ironwork

27

now backed to screen the excavations. She stopped at the Springers' house to let Denise out.

"Forgot to tell you," Denise said. "We're going to have supper here. Special welcome for you. Reid and I will walk up and collect you at seven—all right?"

"Yes, lovely."

On past Denise's house, bright with lights, the drive filled with cars—another of their frequent parties, Philippa surmised. She drove on to the last house. She was home.

She put the car into the garage, took out her suitcases and walked past the door which was meant to give direct access to the hall but was always blocked by the piles of empty cartons which her mother kept in the belief that they would one day come in useful. She went up the stone steps to the front door, which as usual was open, her mother being of the opinion that there was nothing inside to attract burglars. She entered the hall, put down her suitcase and called.

"Mother, I'm here."

The door of the drawing room opened; her mother stood on the threshold, and the past two years fell away as though they had been a rather confusing dream. Here, she saw thankfully, there was no change. Here was her mother's calm, lovely, nunlike face, hair drawn back into a bun. The same, or a similar, shirtwaist dress, the same low-heeled shoes. And the same low, quiet, musical voice.

"Philippa, darling . . ."

2

During her visit to Canada—her first prolonged absence from home—Philippa had had to answer a great many questions about her mother. Distant relations, many of whom had years ago visited her at the Ridge, wanted news of her, and Philippa had done her best to supply it. Yes, she said, her mother was a very contented person; she loved her home and seldom left it. No, she didn't like cooking. (How to explain that as long as she could remember her mother's principal diet had consisted of biscuits and cheese, fruits in season, and salads surrounding a hard boiled egg?) Yes, her mother liked to work in the garden, but hadn't what were called green fingers. (No need to add that her mother thought that weeds gave a garden a pleasant touch of nature.) No, she never did knitting or crochet or embroidery. (No need to recall the cardigans that failed to meet in front, the sweaters that sagged to the knees, the gloves with seven fingers.) Yes, she liked animals but did not keep pets. No, she was not a great reader. No, she seldom looked at television.

The questioners had looked puzzled, but none had posed the obvious question: What did she do with herself all day? It would have taken a long time to tell them. Philippa only said that, no, her mother was never bored.

The questions had led her to attempt some kind of assessment of her mother. There were, she concluded, mothers and mothers. There were mothers, for example, who were more domesticated, who could cook or sew or help with one's homework. There were mothers who occasionally looked at fashion magazines and brought their clothes up to date, or changed their hair style. There were even mothers who took an interest in their daughters' lives, who advised them, who discussed their problems.

Other mothers, better mothers. She would settle, she decided, for the one she had. Detached, but warm hearted and affectionate. Uninterfering; ready to give unobtrusive help to those in trouble, but with an irrepressible tendency to lightness of heart. A mother unlike other mothers . . .

And now she was home, and her mother looked exactly as she had looked when she went away.

They kissed, and her mother stepped back to study her.

"You look well, darling. I hope they told you how pretty you are?"

"Some of the time." She followed her mother into the drawing room. "Why did you go and catch flu?"

"It was nothing. I would have gone to London to meet you if the doctor hadn't fussed. He's getting very doddery, but of course he'll go on till he drops. Is that all the luggage you brought?"

"That's what Mrs. Beetham asked me in the train."

"She was on your train?"

"Both of them. I was in their compartment."

"Awful for you. I suppose she grumbled? She always grumbles, but now she's really got something to grumble about."

Philippa was looking round the room. It was large, and could not be called overfurnished: some comfortable sofas and chairs, one or two small low tables, bookshelves. At the far end was a double door, seldom closed, which led into what had once been a study but which Mrs. Lyle had made into a kitchen. In it could be seen a wide plastic-covered counter, a stove and a sink, and washing, and washing-up, machines. In the centre was a small round table covered with a blue checked cloth. On it were teacups, some jam tarts and a plate of scones. Philippa raised her eyebrows.

"Am I expected to eat all those?"

"Mr. Armitage brought the tarts—he made them himself. He said it's the first time he ever experimented with pastry."

"And the scones?"

"I made those. I found an old packet of scone mixture and tried it out—they look good, don't they?"

"They'd look better if they'd risen. Did you heat the oven before putting them in?"

"Of course I did. It told you to, on the packet."

Philippa turned and moved towards one of the drawing room windows. Her mother put out a hand and halted her.

"Not yet, Phil, please. Tea first. Once I get to a window and start looking out, I lose count of time. I can't tell you how many hours I've spent these past two years, just looking down at what's been going on. Let's have tea while it's hot—then you can look outside. Sit down and I'll make it."

"You sit down and I'll make it."

"I've got thousands of questions to ask you."

Philippa made the tea and carried the tray to the table.

"Go ahead and ask," she invited.

"Does it feel strange to be back?"

"No. In fact"—she spoke in a tone that held surprise and a touch of uneasiness—"I don't feel as though I've been away."

"I liked the look of Dudley from the snaps. Now tell me what he's like."

Philippa, preparing to answer this, sat recalling her fiancé. To her surprise, he did not spring immediately to

31

mind. Puzzled, and in growing dismay, she tried to bring to her mind his features, his voice. She had seen him not so many hours ago. He had driven her to the airport and she had watched him driving away. Now it seemed to her that he had driven so far out of sight that he had left little trace of himself behind.

"He's . . . he's nice," she said lamely at last. "You'll have to wait and decide for yourself what you think of him."

This, to her relief, seemed enough for her mother.

"Next question. How did you get on with your father?"

"Pretty well."

"Did you like him?"

"Yes. I didn't see a great deal of him. The first year, as you know, I went round taking a look at Canada. There's a lot of it to get round. After that I needed money, so I took any odd secretarial job I was offered —so long as I was well paid."

"I'm glad you went to see all my old aunts. I haven't seen them for over thirty years, but I liked them when they came over here. What's your father's wife like?"

"Dressy. Good looking. A bit overweight."

"Do they get on?"

"They bicker a bit."

"Did you see many of his paintings? Can you explain why he was so unsuccessful here and why he's done so well over there?"

Philippa refilled the cups.

"He stopped doing those awful portraits, for one thing. He calls himself a landscape painter, but the landscapes are on a vast scale—huge canvases covered with prairies and forests and wild mountains. He says it's how the early settlers saw the country. They sell well."

"What does she do?"

"She goes out a lot—he doesn't. He has his friends round for bridge; she goes out and visits her own set. She runs a kind of mobile library and drives round the rural districts. Sometimes I wonder . . . but I don't want to be catty."

"Why not?"

"I wondered if it was a sort of cover. She was never very specific about where she'd been, and the books never seemed to have been touched."

"Which would account for her having put up with your father for so long. Fourteen years, isn't it? I only had nine. Did he ever talk about me?"

"Only to explain why he made up his mind to leave you. I didn't point out that he hadn't exactly left you: he'd only left you behind."

"I suppose she makes him more comfortable than I did. It always used to amaze me that although he knew what a wandering life I'd had with my parents, he expected me to know how to run a house."

"The people I talked to over there wouldn't believe that you've lived in this house for so long and had hardly ever left it."

"I suppose they wouldn't. They wouldn't know about all those years I spent with parents who travelled round acting Shakespeare in a fourth-rate company, who always promised they were going to retire and buy another house, but never did. From town to town, morning school with the other theatrical children, one small case containing all one's possessions. Moving, moving, moving. And then a husband who lived in a studio in London and said we'd never leave it—but we did, because he turned out to be a rover, too. In all those years, I dreamed of having a settled home. Now I've got it and I'm determined to stay in it."

"What made my father buy this plot of land?"

"He thought the Ridge would be a good address to

33

which sitters would come for portraits. There was a kind of fashion for portraits when we came here—prosperous tradesmen were hanging their likenesses over the parlour fireplace, and having their wives painted to impress visitors. Your father said it was a good place to settle, so our furniture was brought down from London and we moved in and you were born—the second baby to be born on the Ridge. Denise was the first. I pictured you growing up and going to school every day with your lunch in a little box . . . but you were hardly through kindergarten when I realised that your father's enthusiasm for the house, for the Ridge, for a non-roving life, had died. He began to talk about Paris—a little apartment on the Left Bank, he said. Or Florence, where he could steep himself in his art. Or perhaps North Africa, for the climate. I've told you all this before, haven't I?"

"Yes. Go on."

"He began going on brief trips here and there—I hoped that would cure his restlessness, but it didn't. The trips got longer and longer, but I was happy because I had a home, a kitchen, a garden, a daughter to play with, to tuck into bed in her own room with the pretty curtains and the muslin cot cover. If I'd believed that your father would ever put down roots anywhere, I would have . . . I was going to say I would have gone on following him round, but that isn't true. Most of the money I had—the money old Uncle Theo left me—went into this house, and all the labour-saving equipment that I'd ever dreamed of. I knew that nothing was going to make me give it up. When your father finally said he was going to settle in Canada, I made up my mind. I paid him the share he'd put into the house and said goodbye, don't ever come back. I'm glad he found another wife—that can't have been difficult; he's good looking and he's successful. Once I even thought he was attractive. Have you come back wishing you had two parents instead of one?''

"No. I liked him, but . . . well, he acted too much, I thought.''

"I know. It wasn't only his sitters who did the posing. Why haven't you eaten those scones?''

"I had one. How long had you had that packet?''

"I forget. Laura Plessey brought it, ages ago, for me to try. It got pushed to the back of a cupboard and lost.''

"Put the scones at the back of the cupboard to get lost. More tea?''

"No, thanks.''

"Then could I go and look out of the window?''

"Yes. Not that window. This one. It's got the best view. That's where I took some snaps to send you, but they didn't come out.''

"If you're still using my old box camera, I don't wonder. It . . . ''

She stopped in mid-sentence, unable to go on. She was standing at the window staring down, eyes wide, mouth open, at what, all her life, had been a spacious and well-tended park. Out of this window she had seen her first snow covering the rosebeds, she had watched the ducks on the miniature pond, seen people strolling along the paths or resting on the long wooden benches. Gone, all of it. Below her, on a level far lower than the park had been, she saw the foundations of a Roman villa which had been built almost two thousand years ago.

For some time, she could only gaze. Then she drew a deep breath.

"I didn't dream . . . ''

Her mother was at her shoulder.

"You can't see the pavement from this house. They haven't uncovered much of it, but it's beautiful, Phil.

35

They think there's more of it, but they're not sure."

"I didn't dream . . . I didn't expect it to look so . . . so finished."

"You missed all the preliminary stages. But there was never what you call rubble. It was fascinating to see how they went about it. I'm not such a fool as to have thought that they'd begin by seizing spades and digging, but I had no idea of the care, the patience, the meticulous way they . . . it was like a military operation. Examination by experts of practically every grain of soil, the fragments of pottery they found all lifted out tenderly, photographs at every stage, trial sections, what they call dissection by layers. And, gradually, there it was—the foundations of a villa. They said it was originally half timbered on stone wall bases. You're looking at the bases now. Isn't it fantastic to think we've been walking about on top of that for about a thousand years?"

"What date is it?"

"They're still not sure, but they think it was four hundred and something, towards the end of the Roman occupation. I went to all the lectures and I bought all the little booklets they brought out. There isn't anything I don't know about Roman generals—just ask me." She paused and then went on in a tone of wonder. "Just think, Philippa, before all this began I believed that William the Conqueror was chapter one of English history. I thought it all began with the Norman Conquest."

"1066 and all that?"

"Yes. But he was *centuries* later. In between the Romans and him there were odds and ends I never dreamt of: Saxons and Vikings and Danes . . ."

"The Dark Ages."

"Yes. Oh, darling, will you please come away from this window? It acts like a kind of magnet. I can't tear

36

myself away. Sit down and answer some more questions.''

Philippa moved reluctantly. She went back to the kitchen and put the teacups into the dishwasher. Then she settled herself in a comfortable chair near her mother.

"Go ahead," she invited.

"Are you missing Canada?"

"No." She paused. "Do you want the truth?"

"Yes."

"It's receded. Why?"

"You're home, that's why. It's only natural that you should—how can I put it?—fall back into place. This was your place, after all, for the whole of your life until you went over there. How much did Denise tell you about Reid and herself?"

"Deadlock, she said. It's a pity she ever moved out of her house."

"It was fatal. It's made it practically impossible for her to go back."

"Do you believe that if she married anyone but Reid her father would let her have the house?"

"Not for a moment. In the first place, he takes the line that a man should take his bride to a home, not occupy his bride's home. Next, he and his wife have made themselves very comfortable and nothing's going to move them. As for her father's views on Reid, he's always looked down his nose at the Springers, just as the Beethams have, but I don't think he cares whom Denise marries as long as he and his wife can stay where they are. Did she tell you that she thought your engagement was a little sudden?"

"Yes."

"I thought it was, too. You'd told us to expect you home soon—and the very next letter said you were engaged."

"What did you expect me to do—lead up to it?"

"No. But you'd hardly mentioned him in previous letters, and you'd certainly said nothing about liking him better than any of the other men you met."

"It wasn't sudden. I wasn't thinking about getting married, that's all. He'd asked me, but I was quite happy to come home and leave things in the air. Then it struck me it would be a bit hard on him—he's been pretty patient about waiting for me to decide whether I was in love with him or not. So I said, all right, but I'd have to go back to England to see my mother. That's all." She frowned. "I think I would have made up my mind earlier, but . . ."

"But?"

"I wasn't sure that he was . . . well, my type. I was afraid he'd be . . . heavy."

"Dull?"

"No, not dull. He's serious, that's all. Steady, solid. He's *good*."

"Religious?"

"No. He's got what I suppose you'd call integrity. I decided that seriousness wasn't such a bad quality. He might take a long time to see a joke, and he's certainly got a life-is-earnest approach, but you can't imagine him ever doing anything mean."

"I'm glad he's coming over. Hearing about him is better than reading about him, but being able to talk to him will be best of all. Did your father seem pleased?"

"His wife certainly was. I think she was beginning to fear I'd settle down with them. Now can I ask some questions?"

"Yes."

"About Ward, principally. I can't believe he's really working. Does he still spend most of his time in this house?"

"He hasn't got much time to spend. He's on the site,

or in town, most of the day. But he comes in every morning to see how I'm getting on."

"His job doesn't sound a full time one with pay."

"It isn't. He took it on because the man who was doing it found it more than he'd expected."

"So what does Ward use for money? When he was spending his holidays with his rich Swedish relations, there was no problem. But now?"

Mrs. Lyle considered the question.

"I don't know," she said at last. "I suppose I've got so used to his hand-to-mouth existence that I don't think about it any more. You could ask him."

"What happened to all those Scandinavian blondes who used to come over to see him?"

"His cousins? They still come over now and then, but they don't stay long. He never took much notice of women, as you know. It was the women who ran after him. That hasn't changed. When those students were here—feminine gender—they went down in droves."

"Odd, isn't it?" Philippa said reflectively. "In Canada, I tried to analyse exactly what it was that attracted them. Not his looks—he just looks run-of-the-mill. Not his money, because he hasn't got any. Not his charm, because he doesn't lay on any. A house, but no furniture. A title, but not one spark of ambition."

"He's just nice, that's all. Why do you have to analyse niceness?"

Philippa might have attempted to tell her, but there were voices in the hall. Visitors.

And that was something else that she had found it difficult to explain to relations in Canada—the fact that there was no need for her mother to go out into the world; the world came to her mother. Not a day passed without someone appearing at the house—for a cup of coffee, for a chat, for advice. They came uninvited and unannounced and were content with whatever attention

39

their hostess was able to give them. She went on, as a rule, doing what she had been doing on their arrival, and they sat watching her, or followed her round the house, happy to have a listener who would never repeat gossip. This they put down to discretion, but Philippa knew that her mother could appear to listen while thinking of several other matters.

Two men, one elderly, one young, were in the doorway.

"Don't get up, don't get up," the elder man begged. "We only dropped in to take a look at Philippa."

"Come in, William. Come and sit down, Justin."

The Armitages, father and son, were accountants with an office in the town. Mr. Armitage had built a large, ugly house next door to the Beethams. His wife, a delicate, fretful woman, had managed it with a succession of daily women, and a nanny to take charge of the small Justin. It was not a well run home; meals were never on time, rooms were untidy, clothes unpressed. Then Mrs. Armitage took to her bed and lost interest in housekeeping.

On her death, there had been no lack of female relations anxious to come and look after the two men. But Mr. Armitage was determined to keep his home to himself. Together, he and his son put the house in order. They shared out the domestic duties and carried them out intelligently and efficiently. They taught themselves how to cook; they did the shopping on the way home from the office and had regular days for doing the laundry. They seemed to be demonstrating that they could do most things that women did, and do them better.

Two less likely candidates for a domestic round could scarcely have been found. Both were heavyweights; both had abundant red hair and craggy countenances. William, barrel-chested, had a splendid baritone which

40

he exercised while working in the house. He loved to sing, and two generations earlier would have appeared at parties with a roll of music under his arm, ready to perform. Today, in an age from which drawing room performers had vanished, he sang to himself.

"Couldn't wait to see you," he told Philippa, in a voice whose volume he tried in vain to turn down. "Would have brought along a nice walnut cake if I'd thought you'd eat it. Light as a feather. I've only just turned my hand to cake making, wasn't interested in it before, because who, in these diet conscious days, wants cakes? But d'you know what? I sell 'em."

"Who buys them?" Mrs. Lyle enquired.

"Old Miss Outhwaite, for her tea shop. They're getting popular. She said they were selling like hot cakes, ha ha ha."

"I don't know how you find time," Mrs. Lyle told him when the china had stopped rattling. "In your office all day, the house to look after—"

"Organisation, that's how it's done. Organisation. We don't fiddle about as you women do. Justin and I go at a job, stick at it and finish it. How do the Canadian housewives go about it, Philippa?"

"The ones I knew," Philippa answered, "seemed to get through the housework in a couple of hours."

"Meals straight from the freezer, I bet."

"Well, some."

"Not fat, cheerful faces round a groaning board, as in my grandmother's day. Except at Mrs. Springer's, of course. Did you find Canada cold?"

"In some places and in certain seasons, yes."

"That's what kept me away. A brother of mine went out there when we were young, and he told me that the first time he took a walk—this was in January—his face froze solid. He went indoors and stayed there till it was time to come back to England, so he didn't get to know

41

much about the country. On paper, mind you, I could pass an exam. We had a Canadian geography master at school and he fed it to us in chunks, such as in the coniferous forest belt are fox, moose, otter and beaver, marmot and marten, mink and lynx, porcupine, musk-rat and ermine and skunk and four, no five, varieties of the Canada goose. Am I talking too much?"

"Yes," said Justin. "You are."

"You ever come across any Red Indians, Philippa? Walking around loose, I mean?"

"I watched Indian dancing and . . . "

"No, not that kind. What happened to all the original ones who wore war paint and went round scalping the settlers? I suppose they were wiped out. What part does your fiancé come from."

"Montreal. But we're going to live in Vancouver."

"Ah. Go west, young man. When are you coming to sample some of my Chinese food?"

"Any time you ask me."

"No use asking your mother. And if you bring it here, she doesn't eat it." He rose reluctantly. "Well, time to go. We only dropped in. I left a pie in the oven."

Justin was still in his chair.

"You've shirked it," he told his father laconically, "I knew you would."

"Shirked what?" Mrs. Lyle asked.

"Nothing, nothing." William spoke in an embarrassed tone. "It's not all that important. Come on, Justin."

"When you've said what you came to say," Justin told him implacably.

"We're waiting," Philippa said.

"It was simply . . . Well, I suppose you saw Denise. She went to Canterbury to meet you, didn't she?"

"Yes."

"And of course she talked about herself and Reid Springer?"

"Yes."

"Well—as I said, this isn't important, but it worried me, and I thought I'd pass it on. I happened to run into her father yesterday. He was at the bar of the pub I look into on the way back from the office. He'd had one or two before I got there, and he was in a talkative mood. Someone asked him if it was true that Denise and Reid were going to get married and he said that as far as he knew, yes, it was true, and he was glad to know she'd made up her mind at last, because there were several things he planned to do to the house to make it more comfortable. I said, as casually as I could, that he wasn't the owner and couldn't do any structural alterations without Denise's say-so. To which he replied, not politely, that he was an architect and there were a number of things he could do without structurally altering anything. I've never been able to stand the fellow. It's not as though I've ever had any dealings with him, but I know a lot more about that wife of his than he thinks I know, or she thinks I know, and I don't trust either of them. I thought I'd like to say a word to Philippa, to see if she couldn't make Denise see that if she doesn't take a stand now, if she marries Reid and goes and lives somewhere else, her father'll make sure that she never gets into the house again."

"I think Denise knows that," Mrs. Lyle said.

William turned to her.

"She doesn't know he's going round the pubs talking openly of what he proposes to do to her house, does she? In a way, I'm sorry for the chap. He never got on with his first wife and he never got on with his daughter and I think he led a lonely sort of life, and I daresay going after all those women when his wife died was a sign of what he'd been missing while she was alive. All the same, he picked a bitch for his second, if you'll excuse me, and I suppose she's at the back of this plan to do what they like with the house. It could be done. He could put up temporary divisions between some of the rooms—oh yes, it could be done. It's small but it's not a bad house and I can see why they're determined to hang on to it. It's a pity we couldn't stop Denise from walking out when she did. And now I've told you, and it sounds a fuss about nothing, but I think it's worth passing on to Denise and Reid. And now we must be off. Come on, Justin.''

Philippa walked to the gate with them. Then she returned to the drawing room, which after one of William's visits always seemed unnaturally silent.

"I'll tell Denise," she said, "but I don't think there's anything she can do."

"No. It was true what William said about her never having got on with her father."

"Did her mother just leave her the house without any indication that it was for her and her only?"

"She was to get the house when she was eighteen. I suppose her mother visualised her marrying a man who could offer her a home."

"Leaving her father to go on living alone in the house?"

"I suppose so. It's very difficult to make arrangements beyond the grave. Poor Denise."

They said no more on the subject. Some time later, Mrs. Lyle remarked that if Philippa had come back loaded with presents for her, she would like to help her to unpack.

"Patience," counselled Philippa. "First, I want to know what you've been doing since I've been away. Besides gazing out of the window and watching the digging.''

"Would you like to come upstairs and see?"

44

"Yes."

She followed her mother up the broad flight of stairs, across a wide landing, along a blue carpeted corridor and into the large, many windowed room which had been her father's studio. For some moments, she stood looking round at the familiar, indescribable chaos that represented years of experiment on her mother's part and answered the question of what she did with her time. Here was the paint—three unopened tins—left over after her assault on the walls of the bathrooms. In a corner, the potter's wheel which had produced such strange, contorted mugs and ash trays. The spinning wheel—one of the most disastrous of the ventures. The carpenter's bench and the three-legged stool—a mere five inches high after its legs had been cut and cut again in an attempt to make them even. The knitting machine bought second hand during the cardigan craze. The hand loom—a disaster from the word go. Here it was, all of it, strewn on the large trestle table or disposed round the walls. Here was the reason that the other rooms of the house were so tidy. Years of well planned beginnings and unsuccessful endings and long, happy hours, days, weeks, months during which her mother remained totally absorbed and contented and creative. Was it, Philippa had sometimes asked herself, an artist in her mother struggling to get out? Text books bought and studied, implements and materials and equipment assembled; earnest preparation followed by indefatigable industry followed by inevitable failure, the unfortunate end products proving that this, perhaps, was not the right craft to have chosen.

"Well," she asked. "What are you on now?"

"I haven't started yet. See those books? They tell you all about book binding. It's *fascinating,* Philippa. What I'm going to do is to use the rubber cement method—you get all the sheets together and shave them

45

down and then you coat them with a layer of rubber cement and it holds the leaves together and you don't have to do any stitching. I want to use leather bindings. I waited until you came home because I thought you might be going up to London and wouldn't mind buying the leather for me. This book gives addresses where you can get the right kind. And I'm going to learn how to do gold lettering and decorations—that's in this book.''

''Mrs. Beetham could show you. She does book binding.''

''If she can, I can.''

It was this conviction, inevitably erroneous, that sent her mother hopefully from project to project. If Mrs. Beetham, so pretentious but so basically silly, could bind books, it shouldn't be too difficult for anyone else.

''Why don't you go to evening classes in the autumn?''

''No. I work better teaching myself—and I hate going out. I had a good idea about Christmas presents. I'm going to cut strips of leather, fringe them and put some gold decoration on them—perhaps the initials of the people I want to give them to. They'll make nice presents, don't you agree?''

Philippa agreed. Most mothers, she thought, would have been planning for their daughter's wedding in June instead of for presents in December—but this was her mother's way, and this was the way she liked her mother.

She glanced at her watch.

''Coming to unpack?''

''Yes.''

Her mother sat on the bed while she opened and emptied the two suitcases. Presents—from herself and from Dudley Errol—were handed over. Then her mother went away and Philippa had a shower and changed. The dress she put on was as simple as the one she had taken off; the Springers did not dress up. She put on a light coat and walked out to the gate and saw Denise and Reid coming up the road to meet her.

"Hello, Reid."

He looked down from his six feet three inches.

"Hi, Phil. How's things?"

"Fine."

"Come on down to the lights where I can see you."

The Springers' small hall was as cluttered as Philippa had always seen it. The hat stand, the bulging anoraks hanging on the walls, the tennis racquets and surf boards and gardening implements left little space for anybody to move. Ronnie and his wife had come with their two children to welcome her—the children, twins of six, not alike but both with a strong look of Ronnie, stood waiting expectantly, their eyes on Philippa.

"In my coat pocket," she told them.

With whoops of delight, they retrieved the small packages she had brought them from Canada.

"How about saying thank you?" their mother asked them—but they were already in the living room, tearing off the wrappings.

A voice hailed them from the kitchen.

"In here, girls. Come and talk to me."

They went into the warm, littered kitchen and the stout form of Mrs. Springer advanced, in her hand a wooden spoon which she held out of the way while she offered Philippa a cheek to kiss.

"Seems no time since you went," she told her. "Why did you go an' fix yourself up with a fellow over there? What was the matter with a nice English chap? Here, let me see you. You don't look a mite different."

"Nor do you."

If she had to choose a second mother, she would have chosen Mrs. Springer. To look at her face, once so

47

pretty, now overstretching its skin, was to see what her daughter Sylvie would become—what Sylvie was already becoming. Or to look at Sylvie was to see the lovely girl who had come to the Ridge twenty-four years ago. From Mrs. Springer had come the easygoing natures of her three sons and her daughter. Hers had been anything but a harsh rule—not harsh enough, people had said. But she had managed to steer her family through the jungle of drugs and drink and promiscuous sex, all of which she regarded as illnesses like measles or chicken pox: they might catch them, but if they did you helped them to get better. She had never forgotten the poverty of her early years, and had kept her children in touch with relations less fortunate than themselves. They had grown up learning to give as well as to receive.

Supper was laid on the square table that took up most of the room. Ronnie and his wife took their places beside the two children. Denise and Reid sat on either side of Philippa; Mrs. Springer was at the head of the table. A place was laid for Sylvie, but Mr. Springer was absent and so was Parry.

"Come'n'get it." Mrs. Springer carried to the table an immense dish of stew in which small dumplings glistened and bubbled between carrots and turnips and onions. There were no pre-dinner drinks and no wine. There was a choice between beer and cider.

"Sylvie'll be down in a minute. She got back late and now she's decorating herself. You didn't expect to see the old man, did you, Phil dear? Or Parry neither. Parry's going to play in that big match in Italy tomorrow, and where Parry's playing, his Dad's watching. He's never missed a game yet, his Dad hasn't, not since Parry got to be famous. You'll see him on the telly, if you look, not that he's much good, he doesn't speak up. They ask him things, and he just mumbles."

Sylvie came in. Her brothers gave her no more than a glance, but Philippa thought that she would have made most men forget their food. She was wearing a tight skirt, and a blouse that was cut not only low but loose and which, to complete the process of revelation, was made of transparent material. Her mother clicked her tongue in disapproval.

"I told Philippa you was dressing," she said. "I see I made a mistake."

Sylvie bent to plant a hearty kiss on Philippa's cheek, leaving a scent of what, in reply to Reid's wrinkled nose, she said was the most expensive perfume on the market.

"You don't have to bring it to supper," he told her. "God, how do your boyfriends stick it?"

"They love it. It turns them on." She drew out her chair and sat down. "I've got to do something to get the smell of that office off me. D'you know what the vans were carrying today? Fish. Great boxes of dripping white fish to collect from Canterbury station and bring over to Montoak. It smelt so high I don't suppose the driver had to bother to steer. Easy with the dumplings, Mum."

Mrs. Springer appeared not to hear this. On the subject of food, her views were deep rooted and unalterable. Good, plain food, she stated to anyone who would listen, was the base of health and strength. Dieting under doctor's orders was all right, but going without food to keep fashionably thin was wicked, and flying in the face of nature. She added another dumpling to Sylvie's portion and refilled Reid's plate for the third time.

"Can't tell you where 'e puts it," she said to Philippa. "'E packs it in like an 'orse, and stays just the same, just a stick of spaghetti. It's been like that all 'is life. You could fatten up the others, but you couldn't put an extra ounce on Reid. I used to take 'im up to the chemist's to get 'im weighed when 'e was a little fellow, before we came to live 'ere, and the chemist would say there must be something wrong—'e was only growing one way. Up.''

The empty dish was removed. Reid fetched from the oven a treacle tart that looked the size of a bicycle wheel. Ronnie leaned back to reach for a packet of cream which was standing on a counter. The pastry was crisp and light, and Reid mashed his on to the oozing treacle and topped the mixture with a generous helping of cream. It was, as always, Philippa noted, perfect food cooked to perfection, food up to the standard of a first class restaurant, and it made no difference that it was served on a plastic cloth and chipped plates.

After the meal, the plates were put into the dish-washer and Sylvie made large mugs of coffee. Ronnie, with some difficulty, got the children down from their grandmother's bedroom, where they had been watching a television programme on her portable set. When they had gone, the others gathered round the larger screen in the living room to watch the news. Mrs. Springer, her hands clasped over her stomach, nodded peacefully in her chair, while Sylvie went into the hall and settled down to making a series of telephone calls.

It was nearly midnight when Philippa and Denise rose to leave. Reid left with them; he was going to drive Denise home. They walked out into a night that was cold, but clear. Far ahead, and not so far above them, they could see the chimneys of the Manor. There were lights in Philippa's house—in the hall, in her mother's bedroom and also, probably forgotten, in the drawing room. On the other side of the Ridge was the Armitage house, the moon beginning to rise behind it. As they passed Denise's house, they saw lights go on upstairs.

"It's a lovely house," Denise said. "People say it's

50

not right for this setting, but I think it's the nicest house on the Ridge.''

"Dunno about the nicest. It's the smallest,'' Reid said. "If it'd been bigger, your father would've had more trouble sticking to it; he wouldn't have been able to claim it was just big enough for him and his wife. As far as I'm concerned, he can have it.''

They were silent until they reached the house at the end of the road. Then Philippa said good night and Reid and Denise turned to go back to the car waiting outside the Springers' house.

"See you tomorrow,'' Denise said. "Reid's flat. Come early.''

"Do you want me to bring any food and drink?''

"No. Got plenty. We won't be eating very early—the men'll all be watching the match. Ward'll be with them. He always eats with us after one of Parry's matches. Reid'll drive him out and you can drive him home. 'Bye.''

3

Philippa, usually a sound sleeper, spent a large part of that night in an attempt to restore Dudley Errol to the place he had occupied in the forefront of her mind less than twenty-four hours ago. She decided at last that this difficulty in summoning him to mind, fitting him into her present surroundings, would lessen as the days went by. It was natural enough, she told herself, that on her return home she would have been drawn back into her own familiar world.

But coming home should not, she thought, have wiped from her mind so many impressions of her visit to Canada. When she had said goodbye to her fiancé, to her father, her stepmother and her newly made friends, she had felt no sense of finality; she would be back among them soon. But now her feeling was that she had been to a theatre and enjoyed the show and decided that it might be worth a second visit   and had then driven away to resume life in the world of reality. And most unreal in that make believe world was Dudley Errol.

She awoke to the sound of pouring rain. Going downstairs, she found that her mother, always an early riser, was dressed and had had her morning coffee. She was wrapping a pile of sandwiches into a neat packet.

"Sandwiches for whom?" she enquired.

"Ward. He dropped in last night while you were at the Springers. He didn't know where he'd be at lunchtime today, so I suggested sandwiches that he could take round with him. Any plans for today?"

"Yes. I want to go over the site."

She spoke from the window of the drawing room, looking down through the rain at a scene which was beginning to fascinate her as much as it did her mother. Inclement as the weather was, there were a number of people moving down there, some working in a group close to the Plesseys' garden, others, in mackintoshes and boots and hoods, moving slowly round the site.

"Ward said there were some models coming down from London today," Mrs. Lyle told her.

"Summer fashions to be photographed against the ruins?"

"I suppose so. Perhaps the rain will make them cancel it. Pity. I would have liked to see the girls—men, too, Ward said—striking attitudes. If you're going over the site when the weather clears, why don't you get Ward to take you round?''

"Why do I need taking round? I can read it all up in those booklets you told me about.''

"Did you get the note I left on the hall table last night?''

"No. Are you sure that's where you put it?''

"Well . . . no.'' Her mother went to investigate and came back holding it. "It was in my room; I must have taken it up by mistake.''

"What does it say?''

"That the Plesseys came. They phoned, but I didn't hear.''

Philippa had long ago decided that her mother had trained herself not to hear the telephone. She believed the instrument to be for outgoing calls only; incoming calls could be, and usually were, from people who had time to waste.

"What did they want?''

"They're going to Canterbury this morning to see a house—they wanted to know if you'd like to go with them.''

"No. I'd have to squeeze into the back of their semi Mini, and Laura would drive, and you know what I think of Laura's driving.''

"Yes, I do. You think it's even worse than mine.''

"Right.''

"Then you'd better ring and tell them you won't go.''

Philippa went into the hall, put the call through and answered all the polite enquiries made by Laura, who then put her on to Selma, who made the same enquiries, to which she made the same answers. She put the receiver down at last with a sigh of relief, heard footsteps entering the hall, and turned to find Ward Rowallen entering.

He came in sideways, using his body to push the door wide enough to admit the large parcel he was carrying. He dropped it on the doorstep, took off his streaming raincoat, shook the drops out on the steps, and then turned and saw her.

He looked at her for some moments before he spoke.

"We . . . ell," he said at last on a long note. "Look who's here."

She stood looking at him, and attempted to say something—anything—a word or two of greeting to match the lightness of his tone. But something seemed to have happened to her vocal chords, and to her eyes. The walls of the hall were receding and then coming slowly back into place. Her mind, wrenched from the present, was going back like a roll of film, recalling picture after picture of the hours she had spent, from her earliest years, with this man. She had left for Canada without any special feeling of regret at parting from him. She had thought of him frequently during the past two years, but there had been no letters between them. There had been no warning that on seeing him again she would react as she was doing now.

Ward. After two years, Ward.

She made a supreme effort, and managed a warm smile and two words.

"Hello, Ward."

Ward had been fifteen when his father died. He inherited a baronet's title and an ancient manor, but very little else.

His father had spent little time in the old house. Neglected for generations, it afforded little protection from wind and weather and even less in the way of comfort; most of the furniture had over the years found its way to the salerooms. Ward had spent most of his holidays with his mother's Swedish relations. On his

54

father's death, he had kept on the old servants who had worked for years at the Manor. Marriage and children had increased the number to eight; they looked after Ward when he came home, and on his departure replaced the dust sheets on what remained of the furniture and retired to their quarters at the rear of the house.

In the past he had never made any attempt to interest himself in the life of the town. He picked up the threads of his association with the younger members of the Ridge on his visits home, but it was only with his closest neighbours, Mrs. Lyle and Philippa, that he had ever been intimate. He was very fond of Mrs. Lyle, and treated her as something between a mother and a sister. With Philippa, he was brotherly.

His homecomings had invariably caused an outbreak of love sickness among the girls of the neighbourhood —a fact that never ceased to surprise Philippa, who could detect in him none of the accepted attributes of the lady killer. His was not a face that could be called handsome: it was only his colouring that was unusual—dark skin, dark hair, thick lashed eyes of a striking blue—but hardly enough, she thought, to arouse so much passion among so many of her school-friends. Even Denise had for a time caught the infection, and Philippa had nursed her until the affair had died for lack of nourishment. Ward had remained unaware of her state and oblivious to her suffering. Philippa put down her own immunity to the fact that throughout her adolescence her hero worship had been directed towards the field sports champions, and her passion spent screaming encouragement to the current record breakers.

She could not imagine Ward in any regular employment. On coming down from Oxford, he had announced that it was time to break his forebears' habit of living on or off the furniture, and had offered his services to a bank owned by the family of one of his friends. This appointment, and two subsequent ones, he gave up in swift succession, finding his employers unsympathetic to his need to spend the summers on a Swedish beach and the winters on the ski slopes. The only money he had ever earned had come from instructing the friends of his cousins to ski or swim. But in the last two years, with the discovery of the Roman villa, the pattern of his life had changed.

He looked now to Philippa as he had when she left home, the only difference being that he was not as deeply sun tanned as he used to be in the past.

He hung up his raincoat, took her by the arm and led her into the drawing room.

"I found this young woman loitering in the hall," he told Mrs. Lyle. "She claims she's related to you." He released Philippa and looked at the packet of sandwiches on the table. "Ham or cheese?"

"Good morning," said Mrs. Lyle.

"Sorry. Good morning, Mrs. Lyle. Good morning, Miss Lyle. Ham or cheese?"

"Ham. But you won't feel like picnicking on a day like this. Why don't you go into a restaurant and have at least a snack lunch?"

"Because the food in this town is substandard. I'm doing my best, as you know, to raise the level of meals offered to unfortunate visitors, but it's uphill work."

"You're trying to do it all too fast," Mrs. Lyle told him. "You can't expect cafés and restaurants to switch to French or Italian or Indian or Chinese cooking overnight—and if they did, they'd lose half their customers."

"Oh no, they wouldn't." He was pouring coffee into the cup that had been put down for Philippa. "Things have changed." He pushed down the bar of the toaster.

"The package tour has widened the culinary consciousness of the English. They go forth in groups, herded into planes and coaches, they're conducted to foreign beaches and bars and left there till it's time to go home. They don't see churches or monuments or tombs, and don't want to. Their only interest, apart from . . . "

Philippa had had time to get herself in hand. She spoke in a protesting tone. "That's my toast you're eating."

"Sorry. As I was saying, their only interest, apart from—"

"Why didn't you have breakfast at home?"

"I did. I worked up an appetite coming down the hill after it. Their only interest, apart from the broiling they give themselves on the beaches, is the local food. They're obliged, for a time, to forgo the roast beef of Old England and eat foreign food. They may not enjoy it, but they come home prattling of pizzas or mushrooms à la Grecque or tripe à la mode de Caen. Their wives, merely to show off, begin to experiment with exotic dishes. It starts as a gimmick and becomes a way of life. Every teenager leaving his thousand pound motorbike on the pavement and walking into a restaurant today can now read a French menu. He . . . "

"Look, that's the last of the coffee," Philippa informed him.

"Make another lot, would you? He's no longer a provincial. He's sophisticated. So it's natural to sweep away the dreary food offered in the town restaurants and get them to appoint chefs and maître d'hôtels and waiters who've been trained to wait." He looked round for some more bread to toast, found that Philippa had cut two slices for herself, and appropriated them. "Progress is slow," he continued, "but we *are* progressing. If you ever went out, I'd take you to dinner at the newly christened Coq d'Or. We had to cheat over the chef—he's the son of old Mrs. Fordham. He's lived in Paris and he attended a Cordon Bleu class until they maltreated lobsters and he left—but the maître d'hôtel can put on an almost genuine French accent and the waiters know what they're doing and we've hung a chain and a key round the neck of the wine steward. Why don't you come, just to see?"

"No, thank you."

"You could take me," suggested Philippa, to her own surprise. "I'm not doing anything tonight or for the next six weeks."

For the first time, he seemed to give her his full attention. His eyes rested on her and she would have given much to know what he was thinking.

"All right," he said at last. "I'll take you. Not tonight—this is the night we all devote to watching Parry Springer shooting goals." He gestured towards the window. "When are you going over the site?"

"Today, if the rain stops."

"Will the models come down to be photographed?" Mrs. Lyle asked him.

"Probably. Having come all the way from London, they'll want to take back some results."

Philippa had made some more toast. She buttered a slice and gave it to him.

"I hear you've got a job," she said. "Making lists of things."

Indignation made him pause before his next bite.

"Making lists? Do you think that's what the job is— making lists? The way you make lists of groceries, like carrots and turnips?"

"They're not groceries. They're greengroceries."

"So you say. What I do is to put on record the finds that . . . Well, I don't suppose it's any use trying to explain until you've seen the ruins." He addressed Mrs.

58

Lyle. "I brought those books you asked for—they're in a carton in the hall. Want them in here?"

"No, thank you. I'll deal with them later."

"Then I'll be on my way."

The door closed behind him, and Philippa recalled that Denise had always said that he and Mrs. Lyle were two of a kind. It was true, she thought. Both had their feet a little way off the ground, both had a casual approach to matters which most people considered important. Both took life lightly.

The door opened again. Ward's head appeared round it.

"Meet you on the site at three," he told Philippa.

The door closed.

"That's if he remembers," Philippa told her mother. "Can I do any shopping for you?"

"No, thank you."

"Want me to fix anything for your lunch?"

"No, thanks. I made myself some sandwiches. They're in the fridge. What did . . . "

The door had opened again.

"Forgot to say congratulations on your engagement. Hope you enjoyed Canada."

"I did, thank you."

This time he did not reappear. Mrs. Lyle reverted to her question: What had Mrs. Springer cooked for supper last night?

"Stew and dumplings. Not slimming, but savoury. Enough meat in the stew to feed a battalion."

"We talk about legions now."

"What are the books in the hall?"

"Leather work and book binding. There may not be much furniture in the Manor, but there are some wonderful old books, some of them with lovely bindings. I wish you had time to look through them—but you're going to be busy until you go away."

59

Not busy with housework, Philippa saw. There was little to be done in the house. Her mother looked after her own bedroom, and was seldom in the drawing room. Philippa cleared the breakfast things, ran the vacuum cleaner round the hall and the drawing room, put a pile of clothes into the washing machine and then went upstairs to tidy her room. She spent the morning writing letters to her father and her fiancé. It was easy to fill two or three pages to her father—she had enjoyed the flight, she was home, her mother was well, the Ridge had changed, the Plesseys were leaving, the site of the Roman villa was something she would need time to get used to, she hoped all was well and she was his affectionate daughter.

To Dudley Errol, she said much the same, but in different terms. She told him, with truth, that she missed him. She did not think he would be reassured to learn that he had faded to a hazy outline with a transatlantic accent, and she could not tell him that when she went to Canada she took her home with her, but on leaving Canada, she had left Canada behind. It was only, she felt, the natural pleasure of finding herself once more in the place to which she belonged. She would have to leave it soon—a prospect that looked less simple than it had done on the other side of the Atlantic, and far less attractive than before she had seen Ward.

She made herself an omelette for lunch, and her mother joined her at the table. After eating, Philippa borrowed the leaflets and booklets of information her mother had amassed, and took a crash course on Roman villas and baths and pavements. Then she went out into an afternoon that was sunny and almost warm, and walked down to the gates and on to the site of the villa.

"We'll do this later." It was Ward speaking. "Come down to the baths first."

They had to walk almost to the end of the site.

"How much do you know about the Roman occupation?" he asked her as they went.

"Hadrian built a wall."

"Is that the sum total?"

"Practically."

"That's about all most of the sightseers know. I suppose you know when the Roman conquest took place?"

"Well, vaguely. There was a sort of preliminary skirmish by Caesar in the year 55 or thereabouts. He couldn't have liked the place, because it was over a century before any more Romans showed up. I'm not surprised. Caesar's description of the natives wasn't reassuring; blue war paint, primitive huts, tribal organisation and human sacrifices. What date was the spread of Christianity?"

"Third century. It was firmly established by the fourth." He halted. "Here's where the baths begin. What you're looking at is what was called the frigidarium, which was a . . ."

" . . . cold bath room, very often with a vaulted ceiling and a large swimming tank."

"Right. If you come along here, you'll see what was called the tepidarium, which was . . ."

" . . . a warm room in which you perspired after taking your clothes off."

"I see you've been taught something about it. Now this, over here, is the calidarium which is . . ."

" . . . the hot room. You had a hot bath in a tub called an alveus, and at the other end of the room there was a thing called a labrum, which was a marble basin for giving yourself a rinse."

"You've been cheating and I've been wasting my time?" he said indignantly.

"No. You'll find it fascinating. There was—is that it

over there?—the sudatorium or laconicum which was where you sweated. Heating came from a furnace from which hot air went under a raised floor—the suspensura—into a chamber called the hypocaustum, and from there it went in tubes here and there. After you'd had your bath, you were scraped with a thing called a strigil, to remove dirt and perspiration. Wouldn't you have thought that after the frigidarium and the tepidarium and the calidarium and so on, you'd hardly need scraping?"

"If you preferred reading it up to being shown over the site, you could have said so and saved me a lot of trouble."

"What trouble?" she enquired mildly. "Walking down from your house?"

"Leaving an important meeting in the middle."

"You should have left it earlier. You missed seeing the models posing as Roman virgins. Very unimaginative; they would have sold far more copies of the magazine if they'd posed while rinsing themselves in the labrums or being scraped with a strigil. Where did you eat your sandwiches?"

"Under a tree outside a pub, when the sun came out. Were you as flippant as this before you went away?"

"You find me flippant?"

"I find you less respectful to your elders—meaning me—than you were when you went away. You used to look up to me, and I don't mean physically. You hung on my every word."

"You didn't throw me many words. Why"—they walked slowly towards the villa—"why, after a lifetime of ease and leisure, have you appointed yourself director of these excavations?"

"It was solely . . . "

" . . . due to you that they discovered the ruins. I know. Denise told me. My mother told me. But why not just let the experts get on with their job, and . . . "

"I wouldn't dream of encroaching on any job any expert was doing. My interest began simply because I realised that all this was going to change the town. As you weren't here when the local excitement began to grow, I can tell you that it was as crude as a gold rush. There were tourists and sightseers to be exploited, and nobody of any weight in the town seemed to care how the exploiting was done. I'd never done anything on the site before I took on the cataloguing. What I did, what I'm still doing and hope to go on doing, is raising the standard of food and accommodation on offer to visitors."

"Is that what the meeting was about?"

"That's what the weekly meetings are about—trying to persuade the local hoteliers—hotelier, there's only one—café owners, boarding house keepers and tradespeople that if the people visiting the site can find decent bed and board in this town, they'll stay in it, instead of driving to Canterbury and spending their money there."

"Powerful competition you're up against. Canterbury's got a cathedral and a Roman burial mound and a ruined Norman keep and Sir Thomas More's head and Sir Thomas à Becket and a cricket week and all that ravaging and capturing by the Danes in the ninth, tenth and eleventh centuries. What do we have that could lure tourists away from all that?"

"Peaceful surroundings, a magnificently excavated Roman villa and baths, fresh food from nearby farms."

"And an ancient manor house. You could charge an entrance fee and buy back all your furniture. If you don't want me to tell you any more about these remains, couldn't we go up and take a look at it?"

"Yes. The Chesters will be glad to see you."

They walked out on to the road and followed the

63

curve past the Springers' house and the Lutons' and finally Philippa's. A short distance beyond this was a wide, stony avenue that led up to the manor on the summit of the hill. As the road ascended, overhanging branches shut out much of the sunlight. To right and left was woodland through which, now and then, they could glimpse on one side the church tower and the chimneys of the town, and on the other, the roofs of the houses on the Ridge.

"There are eight Chesters now, aren't there?" she asked as they walked slowly up the sloping, sheltered approach.

"Yes. Old Chester, plus son, plus son's wife plus five grandchildren. A nice family—it was the best idea I ever had, persuading them to come here. Old Chester could never have looked after the place alone."

"But you have to feed them and keep them, which must be expensive—haven't we always thought of you as on the bread line?"

"It's never been as bad as that. I've always had my mother's money. My father had it till he died; now it's mine. It's not much, but it makes all the difference."

"All the difference between having to work, and not having to work?"

"Quite right. Enough to keep me and the eight Chesters."

"Enough to keep your wife and eight children?"

"How does one know?" He picked up a pine cone, threw it into the air and hit it with his fist as it came down. "It all depends, doesn't it? If my wife's an heiress, where's the problem? Naturally, I'll look for one—an heiress—when I feel matrimonially inclined. Most of the men of my family seemed to have a fatal attraction for rich brides—but an ancient manor needs a lot of upkeep. What with upkeep, and buying back the furniture and staffing the place with several generations

64

of Chesters, the heiress's money never went far. Just after you went to Canada, I was given a grant toward roof repairs. Not a large grant—the building isn't in the national monument category. But it helped."

They had walked slowly round a curve. The trees were now bordering a drive that ended in a large courtyard. Beyond was the Manor. Philippa stood and looked at it for some time without speaking.

"It's beautiful," she said at last. "It's . . . "

Something in the scene—the ancient house, the background of trees, the half ruined adjoining chapel with its crooked cross—gave her a sudden feeling of compassion that made it difficult for her to speak.

"Had you forgotten it?" he asked.

"No. Oh no. But I didn't realise how much . . . "

"How much it needs a facelift? It leaks in places, but it still affords shelter. Does it make you feel sad?"

"Yes. Find that heiress soon."

"I'll do my best. Remember the times we all used to come up here and rampage round the grounds?"

"Yes."

"I always thought—we all thought—you'd come back to us. When you wrote and said you were engaged, a kind of tremor went round the Ridge. We'd all taken you for granted. I'd always had you fixed in my mind as someone who had always been here and would always be here. I still can't believe you're going. I hate the idea."

The lightness had left his tone. He was speaking, she knew, seriously. She would almost have said he was speaking from the heart. She felt her own heart beating fast, and gazed fixedly at the view until she could steady herself. Then she faced him.

"Can we go inside?"

A large, empty entrance hall, two shallow marble steps, an inner hall, arches to right and left. All, she knew, additions made to the original house. Then the central hall, echoing, uncurtained, uncarpeted, with a minimum of furniture. It was meticulously clean; the floors shone, the window panes were clear.

"I don't use this," he said unnecessarily. "I've fixed up two rooms that used to be my father's study and dressing room. In here."

He had made these comfortable, at any rate. They were rooms which looked out on to the woods at the back of the manor, rooms she had never seen, for his friends had rarely entered the house; there was too much to amuse them outside.

They stood at one of the windows. To their right, somewhere far below, was the Roman villa, but she could believe at this moment that nothing had changed, that he had never discovered Roman remains, that she had never been to Canada.

He spoke out of a long, comfortable silence.

"Pity you're marrying so far away. It would have been nice for your mother to have you rather more within reach."

"She won't be lonely."

"No," he agreed. "She won't be bored, either. What's your fiancé like?"

"You'll see him; he's coming over."

"So your mother told me. A lawyer, she said."

"Yes. We're going to live in Vancouver."

"Then you won't be near your father either. I remember him quite well. My father didn't like him, I don't quite know why—I don't think he saw him more than two or three times. I gather he's given up portrait painting."

"Yes."

"How did you meet this fellow—what's his name?"

"Dudley Errol. I met him when I went with my father to a picture exhibition in Montreal. He—Dudley

66

—is a sort of amateur artist, and he likes going to exhibitions. My father knew him, and asked him back for a drink. Then I didn't see him for some months. Then he rang up and asked me out to dinner.''

"And so it began?''

"So it began.''

"And he fell in love, and you fell in love?''

"He asked me to marry him, and I said I would.''

"That doesn't answer my question.''

But the question was not repeated.

They saw, coming through the wood, a man and three large dogs. Ward leaned out and whistled, and the animals came bounding to the house, entered it, barking hysterically, and scrambled across the slippery floor to throw themselves on him. Two were young, the third was well known to Philippa.

"Hello, Carlo.''

She held out a hand, but to her surprise the dog hesitated before coming up to her.

"Don't tell me you've forgotten me!'' she exclaimed in surprise. "It isn't so long.''

He began licking her hand, and Ward smiled.

"Not so long, but you've changed. He had to have a moment to place you.''

"Changed? How?''

"I'm trying to decide. I'll have to think it over, like Carlo.'' He paused. "It could be, of course, that I didn't take a clear look at you before.''

"You were usually on your way to Sweden. Don't you ever go there now?''

"I was there last autumn, but the cousins I knew best have all married and can't roam free any more. It's not as much fun as it used to be. And I now find things in this place more interesting than I used to. How old is this Errol?''

"Thirty-two.''

"What does he do, besides his job and his painting?"

"Games. He's got a cottage up in the mountains and he goes up sometimes for a weekend's skiing."

"The good life. Domesticated?"

"I don't know." She walked slowly to the door, and he followed her. "Instead of talking about me," she said, "could we talk about Denise and Reid? I'm worried about them."

"Why? They're enjoying the good life, too."

"Reid wants to get married, but she's . . . "

"I know. Dragging her feet because she wants her father to let them have the house. Pure pigheadedness. Reid ought to stop listening to her and look for a place of their own. That flat over his garage is all right for him, but the two of them couldn't settle down in it. If he hasn't the money to buy a flat or a house, his father would lend it to him. Do you want to see the Chesters?"

"Yes."

The old butler's greeting to her was paternal. He had been one of her favourites while she was still in her infancy. The rest of the little family group gathered round, and she admired the baby who had not been there when she left for Canada. Then, with the dogs in attendance, they left the house. Ward led her to the point on the edge of the wood from where they could look down at the whole range of the excavations.

"I'm surprised that none of the photographers found their way up here to take an overall view," he said. "All they did was take it in sections and join it up." He gave her the puzzled look he had worn in the house. "Yes, you've changed."

"People do, don't they? Two years is . . . well, two years."

"Perhaps I should have visited my oculist more regularly. Did you fall in love all at once?"

"No."

"Did he?"

"I don't think so. He met me and remembered me, that's all. Haven't you ever kept a girl in mind, just in case you come across her again? No. Silly question. You couldn't have kept them in mind, because none of them made any impression. Perhaps it was a sort of defence mechanism—a realisation that there were too many of them to cope with. Nobody could ever accuse you of encouraging them."

"What did I have to encourage them with? A title and a half derelict house and a yearly income a docker or a train driver would laugh at . . . Did you always have this beautiful skin?"

"Always, with perhaps a year's interval when I was about fifteen. Haven't you got to go back to your cataloguing?"

"I'm doing it . . . Were your eyes always this shade of blue?"

"I'll check with my mother." She was walking back to the avenue. "Everybody—except Denise and myself—seems to be watching Parry Springer's match this evening."

"Not everybody. His mother doesn't like watching, so she goes and sits with your mother, who isn't interested in watching soccer or any other sport. The Springer family sit riveted to their own set. The Chesters gather round theirs. I join the Springers because any comments they make during the game are worth listening to."

"I'm helping Denise with the supper."

"Good. You can drive me back home."

The match had begun when she left the house. Mrs. Springer was already installed in the drawing room, in a comfortable chair with her feet on a low stool.

"Brought along a bit of mending," she told Mrs.

Lyle on her arrival. "Hope you don't mind. You going along next door to watch?" she asked Philippa.

"No. I'm going to make supper with Denise."

"You'll find the streets empty. Everybody inside—all those millions over here and on the continent, watching twenty-two men kicking a ball around a field. Makes you think, don't it? If you ask me, it's not a game any more, it's just big business and in a way I wish Parry'd never got into it, but his Dad says 'e'll 'ave enough money to give it up at an age when most men 'ave only just got started. Are you going out straight away, dearie, or would you 'ave time to make me a nice cupper?"

"I'm sorry—I forgot to ask you." Mrs. Lyle sounded distressed. "I'll make it."

"Oh no, you won't," Mrs. Springer said decisively. "You'll sit there and talk to me, and Phil can do it. I'm not one of those who believe in wearing the old ones out first."

Philippa, making the tea, tried to guess how many cups Mrs. Springer drank in the course of a day. It was, she knew, the only thing that made her stop work and sit down for ten minutes.

"Thanks, dearie. Do they drink much o' this in Canada?"

"Coffee, mostly."

"I never touch it. The nicest bit of my day is when I take my first cupper in the morning. When I was younger, and used to go travelling with my old man, I took our tea caddy with us, and I got boiling water in a flask and made our own. 'E said it was wrong, you shouldn't go to foreign places and do what you do at home, but I suppose I was too old to change. I only liked it when we took the kids, and we only went to places near 'ome. Belgium, mostly—those nice beaches."

"You took me once," Philippa reminded her.

"That's right, dearie, we did. And what I'm always saying: I'm glad we got our travelling over when things was still quiet, and kids behaved like kids. Nowadays, they don't go with Mum and Dad, oh no. They buy a shining great motorbike and tie a girl on the back and go roarin' off camping in them little tents, how they fit in is a wonder. And all the money in the world to spend. Funny, isn't it, the way it's the youngsters who pull in the big money nowadays? And do they save it, like we taught Reid and Ron and Parry? Not they. Time and time again I say to my old man that it wasn't too easy, bringing up our kids, but I'm glad we 'aven't got to do it today, not with the world the way it is. I don't read the papers, not any more, I get too upset reading about all those bombs going off and killing innocent people. If there's a dirtier way of fighting, tell me what it is—'ide your bomb and make a run for it. And you can't tell me that they're all people with what they call a cause. 'arf of them are young thugs making bombs in back yards, and don't tell me they 'aven't got their ideas off the telly, because it's wicked what they put on and then they pretend they don't know why there are riots all over the place."

"Mother doesn't read the papers, either," Philippa said.

"Quite right too. I 'ope you'll be able to bring your children up to make 'em turn out decent, like ours. Just luck, their Dad says, but it wasn't, not all of it. It was a lot to do with keeping them busy outside school time. It was lucky Dad was a builder and they could 'ang round learning about bricklaying and that. Eight years old, Reid was, when 'e built 'is first house. Three feet 'igh, and it let the rain in, but it was a good job all the same, and 'e did it all 'imself."

Mrs. Lyle, a chair drawn up to the table, was

listening, or not listening, her hands busy sorting a drawerful of faded snapshots. Philippa left the two women and drove to the flat which Reid had built above the garage in which he kept his vans. She went up the outside staircase, opened the door at the top and found Denise in an apron, inspecting the contents of the saucepans on the stove. There was a strong smell of spices.

"Come in," she said. "You're later than I expected."

"I was listening to Mrs. Springer. Nonstop, but most of it quite good sense."

"The trouble, is, nobody listens any more. Any news of the score?"

"No. Shall I switch on and find out?"

"Let's wait. We'll get it all when they arrive."

"What are you cooking?"

"Mixed vegetables. You can make the salad if you like—it's all there, ready. Leave the garlic separate, but chop some up and put it on that steak. I won't start grilling it until I hear them arrive. And you could open that bottle of wine. Reid and I aren't winers, but Ward is. Did he take you over the remains?"

"Only part. I wanted to go up and see the house. He seems to have made himself comfortable in those three rooms."

"It's funny, isn't it? He behaves as though he's here to stay, but what's there to stay for, unless he gets himself a proper job—and what job could he get in this place that would give him enough to live on? Live on properly, I mean. I hate to think of his future. If he ever did get any money, Reid said it would have to go in repairs to the house. Want to listen to music?"

"Wouldn't mind."

"There's a new recording of Beethoven's Third Piano Concerto—Reids says it's the best yet."

Philippa put it on, and they went on with preparations for the meal and laid a blue cloth on the table and put out stainless steel knives and forks and paper napkins. When the two men arrived, the last movement of the concerto was coming to an end.

"What d'you think of my love nest?" Reid asked Philippa.

"I think it's very nice, but it's not nice enough for you both to settle down in."

"You mean when we get married? You'd better talk to Denise about that."

"It's no use talking to Denise," Ward said. He was lying on the edge of the large bed, his head on his clasped hands. "She was always impervious to good advice, and she's closed her mind to sensible ideas. If Reid waits for her to make a decision, he'll be an octogenarian before he's a husband. He'd better find himself a nice house and let Mr. Luton and his wife have the one on the Ridge. Do you keep anything in the way of aperitifs, Denise?"

"Oh, yes. I bought a bottle of sherry. It was terribly expensive."

"And totally unnecessary," added Reid. "Did you buy that bottle of wine, too?"

"Yes. But Ward will say it isn't the proper room temperature."

"Why all the fuss?" Reid demanded. "He thinks enough of himself as it is. I'm waiting for him to claim that he's a direct descendant of the Romans who lived in that villa."

"My ancestors," said Ward, "were all men of Kent. They were the natives that Caesar found so primitive."

"Speaking of your ancestors"—Reid was putting chairs round the table—"I've never understood how it was that one of them managed to get himself drowned. Drowned in what?"

"There was a stream which . . . "

73

"Yeah, I know about that. But there wasn't much of it, and it tailed off at the Plesseys' garden and gave them the idea of building Japanese bridges and so on. But how could anyone drown in it?"

"By falling into it head first off a bridge," Ward explained.

"There was a bridge?"

"Once, yes. If anyone wanted to get up to the Manor without giving themselves the trouble of going round to the avenue, they had to cross the stream. There was a small wooden bridge which, like everything else the family owned, was in pretty poor condition. It collapsed while the ninth baronet was crossing it, and he went in head first, as I said, and they found him there, dead."

"When was that, exactly?" Denise asked.

"Exactly? It was in the year eighteen hundred and eighty. You can see his portrait in the gallery, fourth from the end on the right as you go in."

"The one with the nasty expression?"

"Yes. He wasn't a pleasant character. All the same, he managed to get two beautiful women to marry him. Do I smell curry sauce?"

"Yes. Put it on the table, will you?" Denise was carrying the steak on a large, hot serving dish. "There are three sauces. Reid won't eat the curry one and I won't eat the mustard one, but there's plenty of the mushroom one. Phil, bring the vegetables, will you?"

They sat down. The dishes were put on the table and they helped themselves.

"Perfect," Ward said after the first bite. "Very expensive meal, with steak the price it is." He took a generous helping of curry sauce. "She's a funny girl, Denise," he told Reid. "Parry, going to be her brother-in-law and she hasn't even asked if his side won."

"All right, did his side win?" Denise asked.

74

"Yes. It was a close thing," Reid told her. "The first goal came from . . . "

"That's the lot," Denise said firmly. "I didn't ask for a sports round-up. I simply wanted to know who won. I'm not a fan."

"Nor was my grandmother up in Selby," Reid said. "First time they sat her down to watch one of Parry's matches, she wanted to know why the players didn't look where they were going." He got up to put on a record. "One reason for moving out of this place," he said, resuming his seat, "is that the acoustics are rotten. What's the use of a first rate recording if it's ruined by bad acoustics?"

"When we're married," Denise observed, "the conversations are going to be pretty one-sided. When he's finished describing every goal in every match, he'll get on to acoustics, and after that he'll go on to van repairs. Which reminds me: Sylvie called. There's a job going out at seven-thirty tomorrow morning and she wants you to let her know which van she's to send."

Philippa looked across the table at Reid.

"What made you think of having a fleet of vans?" she asked.

"Didn't Denise tell you?"

"Not in much detail."

"It was Mum started me off, in a way. She wanted to send a sideboard into town to be overhauled, and it wouldn't fit into any car we had, so I said I'd try and borrow a van. No vans. I got so mad trying to transport that bloody sideboard that in the end I bought a van—and then found half a dozen people offering me money to fetch and carry stuff for them. Denise began to keep a list. They kept coming—not only old girls wanting to ship sideboards, but fruit growers who wanted to send their stuff in a hurry to the Canterbury markets, and hadn't their own trucks. Trunks for kids going to school that wouldn't fit on the family Mini and couldn't be sent by train because there was a strike. We had kids who were getting up miniature Tour of Kent bicycle competitions and who wanted their bikes taken to the starting point. We had schools wanting camping gear carried to the camp site. We had animals—puppies, mostly—sold and going to new owners and too nervous to be sent alone, so the owner came in the van too. We carried all the instruments for the Montoak Orchestra all the way to the festival in London. It got so that someone had to stay on the phone, and I bought two more vans and tried to get Ron to drive one, but he wouldn't on account of his wife saying no. So I drove one and two out-of-work pals of mine drove the others, and then Sylvie said she'd take over the office and run it. It was her idea to get us all into uniform—she said we'd look more professional. Now we're in dark green, like the vans, and we've got RSST—Reid Springer Swift Transport—on the front of our shirts and the sides of the vans and we're in business. Any more questions? If not, any more steak?''

When they had eaten, they cleared away the dishes and Reid washed them while the others dried them and put them away. Then they settled down, replete and lethargic, to listen to Reid's records until Philippa rose to say it was time she went home.

She and Ward found that there had been a fall of rain that had left the pavements wet and turned the branches into shower baths operated by gusts of wind. Now and then the clouds parted to give a glimpse of an almost full moon. They reached the car, and Ward took the wheel, as he had always done when they drove together.

"I'll do the driving," he said. "In an emergency, you'll forget that you're no longer driving on the wrong

76

side of the road. Does your father still go in for expensive sports cars?''

"No. He's got a Japanese car with an odd name. He changes it every year.''

"And your fiancé? These polite enquiries,'' he explained, "are to mask my pleasure at finding myself alone with you. Let's recall the happy past.''

"Why? I'd rather go home and get some sleep.''

"You have years and years ahead of you in which to sleep. I've only got these last weeks to relive our old intimacies and gather some last happy memories to comfort me when you've gone.''

"What do you call old intimacies?'' she enquired.

"Those games we used to play. Innocent enough on the surface, perhaps, but . . . ''

"When you were home, which wasn't often, you joined in the teenage romps.''

"We grew up together. At this moment, we're passing a tree from whose topmost branches I once had to rescue you. You went up after a cat. The cat came down with the greatest of ease, but you were stuck. I went up after you, gathered you in my arms and gently carried you . . . ''

"You told me that if I was fool enough to get up, I ought to be fool enough to get down again. You came halfway up, told me to put my feet on your shoulders, and I finished up on my back in the mud. Next intimacy?''

"There was the time we played that murder game on a night like this, only drier, and by some freak of fate, chose the same hiding place in the hollow tree in the avenue. There was scarcely room for one. You clung to me, your body soft against mine, you . . . ''

"I was there first. You tried to squeeze in, couldn't, pulled me out and left me in full view of Ronnie Springer. Next?''

77

"What about the time we organised carol singing and you felt cold and I took off my plaid muffler and wrapped it round your neck and put my arms round you to . . . "

"You weren't there. You'd gone to Sweden."

"Well, I *feel* as though I'd been there. All I'm asking you now is to recreate, while you're here for the last time, those old happy days. You'll soon be leaving—for good. When I say for good, I speak in a time sense. In every other way I don't feel it's for good at all. You belong here."

"I belonged. Past tense . . . This is not the way home."

"And hasn't been for the last four miles. That shows your mind wasn't on the road. We've passed through Montoak and we're approaching its bosky surroundings. As I was saying, you belong here. Whatever this Ridge is or was, the families on it made it a kind of community."

"Of which you were never a member. And you weren't on the Ridge, you were above it. You were here long before the Ridge was thought of. Not you, but your father and all his fathers. I may have belonged, but you never did. Now you appear to have put down a few roots in the Roman dig, and I'm glad, and I hope you stay and I hope that when I've gone, you'll go on seeing my mother and let me know that she's all right. But don't try and fill in my last weeks by pretending that . . . "

He stopped the car, turned to her and spoke in amazement.

"Pretending? My God, who said I was pretending?"

"I did. I don't understand what you're doing, but I'd rather you didn't."

"I was merely trying to tell you, in my poetic way, that I'd come to a late, too late realisation that you're a

78

beautiful and desirable woman. I spent most of last night in a fever of regret that I—that we—had let you leave us and go away and marry a man none of us knew or would ever know. I asked you if you'd changed. You haven't. I'm the one who's changed—from a self absorbed, pleasure seeking, blind-as-a-bat specimen into someone who sees you not only as you now are, but also as the small girl, the teenager, the business girl, the grown-up I've watched all these years. I wondered, last night, if I was deficient in whatever it is that makes for virility. I never felt any interest in any girl, perhaps because most of the girls I met in Sweden and other places abroad were—like myself—whizzing down ski slopes or practising underwater strokes. I didn't think of marriage because what was there to offer a wife? A peppercorn income and a decaying manor. I was happy the way I was, happy when they started uncovering the Roman villa, happy in trying to bring this town up-to-date. Now I'm no longer happy because the sight of you has started a train of reactions which leave me feeling like . . . like a man standing on a platform watching the last train go out of sight."

"Poetic is right."

"Poetic or not, those are my sentiments. All I ask is some small compensating companionship, a few memories that I can live on when you've gone away, something to make me feel that I did at least share something with you even though it was too late."

"Your request will be filed and given due consideration. Now could we go home?"

"Presently. You were never—or were you?—in love before you met him?"

"Not seriously."

"By which you mean that you were perhaps carried away at times by a favourite tune or by someone who danced extra well."

"We all go through moments like those."

"I didn't. Will you at least agree that after having roused these feelings in me you should do something to alleviate them?"

"I won't even agree that I've roused feelings in you. You've just said that we grew up together—that means that I know you pretty well. And in case you've forgotten, there's another man with roused feelings, and . . . "

"I know. Loyalty. I'm not asking you to do anything he wouldn't do. And you might owe him loyalty, but I don't. I don't owe him anything. He shouldn't begrudge me a week or two of your company. You might even find that I have some good qualities that he lacks."

"When I said let's go home, we went home."

"More fool he. Do you think I haven't got him in mind even more than you have? You don't have to remind me that he's an insurmountable barrier between us. I can feel him here now, on guard. Can't you?"

She would have given much to say that she could. But she knew, and the knowledge was bringing her close to panic, that he was no nearer now than he had been when he left her at the airport.

Ward started the car and drove reluctantly homeward.

"At least," he said, as they passed through the deserted streets of the town, "you could give me some of your time while you're here. Or are you too busy assembling your trousseau?"

"Trousseaux are out."

"My grandmother took with her, as a bride, an average of fifty pairs of everything, from sheets to stockings to gloves. I shall expect my bride, if and when, to come as fully equipped. If I'd made love to you before you'd left for Canada, how would you have responded?"

80

"I'll think it over tonight and let you know. Look— pedestrians."

There could be no mistaking the two silhouettes, one so tall, one so short—they were the two Plessey sisters.

Their names, as Laura, the elder, always pointed out to new acquaintances, made identification easy. "L for Laura, L for long," she explained with her too frequent toothy smile. "S for Selma, S for short. You see."

Seeing did not make conversing with them any easier. Selma barely topped five feet, while Laura was over six. For their friends of average height, this entailed an exhausting neck bending or neck stretching exercise. Reid Springer once pointed out that the two were like an uncompleted range-finding manoeuvre: first salvo, too far; second salvo, too near; the third salvo would be bang-on. But there had been no third salvo. Laura and Selma were the only children, and their father, first and last Viscount Brinessing, was long dead.

During their early days on the Ridge, the sisters had been the object of much uncomplimentary comment. Their clothes were made of drab but durable material, Selma's too large and Laura's too small, so that it was believed that Laura handed her outworn garments down to her sister, while Selma handed hers up to Laura.

In spite of Laura's advantage in height, it was the diminutive Selma who was the stronger character, her attitude towards her sister being that of a kind but firm governess. The deep affection between them could not be doubted.

Mrs. Beetham had on their arrival done her best to give them what she called a lead. She had offered to put them up for the Political Club, the Geographical Society and the Historical Society and the Shakespeare Reading Group. The sisters, grateful but elusive, became instead members of the Glee Club and—after some hesitation until it was explained to them that there were no nudist connotations—the Nature Walkers. They had sat ineffectively on several committees in the town, and had come in time to be regarded as odd, but harmless. It was only after they had accepted the post of joint Heads at the newly opened Nursery School that their position in the community changed. Unlikely candidates as they had appeared to be, their appointment proved a miracle of good casting. Bypassing pothooks and percussion bands, the two turned the classes into impromptu music and drama sessions, each term producing plays and cantatas at which their pupils showed such marked talent that gratified parents went hurrying up to theatrical agents in London to announce that a star had been born.

Ward stopped the car and got out.

"What are you doing so far from home at this hour?" he asked.

Laura giggled.

"We've been dining with William and Justin. Such a *delicious* meal!"

"They should have been watching the match."

"Oh, they did, they did! They telephoned as soon as it was over. Parry Springer won, didn't he?"

"With the help of ten others, yes."

"Now I suppose they'll sell him to another team for a lot of money," Selma prophesied. "How successful he has been! Do you think he's *happy*?"

"He keeps his fans happy. He . . . "

He stopped. Laura had given a gasp of dismay and was hurrying round to address Philippa.

"My dear, *dear* child! Here we are talking about football, and completely forgetting that we haven't spoken to you since you came home."

"Except on the phone," Philippa reminded her.

"That didn't count. It shows that we feel you've never been away. How are you, Philippa, dear?"

Philippa got out of the car and received a soft peck on the cheek from both sisters. There was no indication that either of them was worrying over their homeless future.

"Justin wanted to see us home," Laura explained, "but we wouldn't hear of it—such a short distance, and you know how we like walking at night, that's to say on such a lovely night as this has turned out to be. The ruins by moonlight. I can't *tell* you how beautiful they look." She turned to Ward. "You know we were going to see you tomorrow, to ask you to do us a favour."

He had done them countless favours in the past—small, careless, unconsidered kindnesses that they had never forgotten and that had given him a secure place in their hearts. His affection for them had begun when as a small boy he had taken to dropping in to see them every Friday when he was at home—Friday was their baking day, and he came away bursting with hot cakes and pastry.

"It's about tomorrow," Selma told him. "We had a letter this morning from my dear mother—she's driving over tomorrow to see the pavement they've found. It would be so kind if you would show it to her—you know so much more about it than my sister or I do. I'm sorry to, as it were, thrust this on you, but as you know, she never gives one notice that she's coming. She would be very glad if you would give her tea at the Manor, as usual. We shall of course take her out to luncheon."

"I'll pick her up and deliver her back to you," Ward promised.

"That's so kind. She has never forgotten how clearly you explained everything when you took her over the remains. And now we must go. It was such a beautiful night that we felt we must take a walk round this

83

side—should I say your side, Philippa!—of the Ridge. Good night, good night.''

''Pity about that,'' Ward said when he had driven on.

''Why?''

''She's a sharp old lady, the Viscountess, more clued up than either of her daughters. She'll see what they haven't seen yet—in fact, what nobody except those whose job it is to know, knows.''

''Which is?''

''That the pavement extends a good deal further than they thought.''

''Is that a . . . Oh!''

''Exactly. Oh!''

She spoke in dismay. ''Is it quite certain?''

''More or less. Anyhow, they're going on with it. If it extends as far as they think it will, hope it will, then . . . Oh! as you said. They won't be able to uncover any more pavement—if there is any more—without under-mining, if not actually digging up, the Japanese garden. I think it might turn out for the best—it's the only thing that could make those two leave their house without regret. The house was just a house. The Japanese garden was much more. It had become a kind of local sight. And not only local. Some of the reporters that came down here recognised it. But that won't prevent the experts from exposing the rest of the pavement.''

''If their mother guesses . . . ''

'' . . . she won't tell them. I think that's the way they grew up: 'Don't tell the girls.' Anything they know, and it isn't much, they had to find out for themselves.''

He drove the car into the garage. They walked to the house and Ward paused.

''Nice hot cup of something for me?'' he asked.

''No. Not tonight.''

''Are you being inhospitable, or are you being loyal?''

84

"Both."

"I'll ask your mother to come to tea with the Viscountess. Will you come too?"

"Yes. Good night."

"Good night."

He took her hand, deposited a light kiss on the palm and went away.

There was a light under the door of her mother's room, but she did not go in. She got ready for bed and then put out the light and lay with the window curtains drawn back, looking out at the night. The drive home had not been conducive to sleep.

The thing to do, she told herself, was not to go on wondering why Dudley Errol had receded from her sight and memory. She had to make an effort to bring him back. And here he came: tall, broad, by any standards good looking, kind, protective. Their first meetings had not made for what for want of a better word she called an impact. But as she grew to know him better, she had thought that he seemed almost like an Englishman, with his quiet drawling voice, his reserved manner and tendency to understate. He had raised no objections to her coming home, merely saying that he would come and fetch her back. She had, she thought, never had any doubts about her feelings for him—but she had made the mistake of trying to move him from his own background and put him against her own.

She had not, until her return, understood how deeply rooted she was in this place. Leaving it to visit her father had not seemed hard. Staying away for two years, she had experienced no feeling of homesickness. Not until her return had she realised that she had never, in spirit, been away.

She had left home once. She would have to leave home again, but Dudley would be with her and once again there would be no feeling of cutting ties. Everything was going to be all right. And this disturbing, unexpected mood of Ward's . . . she could deal with that. She could hardly avoid him, but she could make him keep within their former friendly frame. She had remained immune to his charm, attraction, whatever it was, for too long to be affected now.

Yes, everything was going to be all right.

4

The Viscountess was nearing seventy, but even at a short distance she could be taken for fifty. Slim, not much taller than her daughter Selma, she was extremely elegant, with an oval, unlined face, misleadingly candid blue eyes and a manner which some people found nauseatingly sugary, but which never failed to have a melting effect on obstructive officials. She made a not-too-well-supported claim to kinship with the Rowallens, which Ward had always regarded as an excuse for visiting the Manor frequently during his father's lifetime in an effort to entrap him into a second marriage.

"Thank God she didn't get him," he had said more than once to Mrs. Lyle. He was saying it again when Philippa came down to breakfast next morning. "A lucky escape for us both."

"Both?" Philippa enquired.

"My father and myself, both. Do you realise she might have been my mother? Good morning, Philippa:

I'm not drinking your coffee. I made my own. I'm here to invite you and your mother formally to do me the honour of having tea with me this afternoon.''

"He's talked me into going," Mrs. Lyle said. "If I don't go, she'll come here to stay heaven knows how long, as she did last time she came to Montoak, while you were in Canada.''

"I left Chester, in fact I left all the Chesters, making elaborate arrangements," Ward said. "There'll be China tea out of what's left of the Sèvres, and cucumber sandwiches and cress sandwiches and a Chester cake which is being made especially for Philippa.''

"Last time I saw her, she was rude to me," Philippa objected.

"Mere routine. She's rude to everybody. I'll keep her looking at the pavement as long as I can, so you won't have to have more than an hour of her.''

Philippa agreed, reluctantly, to go, and it proved in some respects a pleasant hour. Tea was laid at the sunny end of the hall, with a view on to trees shading carpets of daffodils and narcissi. The Viscountess seated herself on a chair that was next on Ward's list of furniture to be sold, and looked out with a sigh.

" 'A crowd, a host of golden daffodils,' '' she murmured.

It was almost the only line of poetry she knew, but she used it with great effect each spring. Philippa hardly heard it, being absorbed in taking in details of the speaker's beautifully cut suit, itself the soft green of spring. Snakeskin shoes on slim, pretty feet and a snakeskin handbag. Not the fashion of the day, when most well dressed women were trousered and booted, but the effect was the one intended—perfect clothes on a perfect figure.

"You *never* change," she told Mrs. Lyle with what

sounded like genuine envy. "You keep *so* young. You make time stand still. How do you *do* it?"

"Starvation," Ward explained. "She lives on air."

Chester, the picture of a perfect butler, brought in the tea. The Viscountess addressed some gracious words to him, and gave another sigh when he had closed the door behind him.

"Such a dear, *dear* old fellow. I feel sad when I see him, Ward, because he makes me think of your father. I've had such happy, *happy* times in this lovely house. I don't think your mother ever loved it as much as I did."

"She spent a lot of money keeping it from falling apart," Ward recalled.

"Ah, keeping up these old houses . . . When I sold the castle after my husband died, I felt heartbroken, but at the same time I realised that I could never, *never* have found the money to keep it up." She accepted a slice of waferthin brown bread and butter. "Though, lately, I've wished that I had never left it. I could have offered my daughters a home now that they've been turned out of that horrid little villa they insisted on renting. They'll regret having left the castle—but nothing would dissuade them. It seemed to me that no sooner was their father buried than they were preparing to leave. I felt at the time, and still feel that it was a very *selfish* thing to do. They knew that I couldn't possibly stay in that vast place all alone. I've never really been comfortable in my present home. When one has been really comfortable, one never really adjusts to harsher conditions. And servants," continued the Viscountess, who had a cook, a butler, two maids and a companion, "are *impossible* to find. Don't you find that?" she asked Mrs. Lyle.

Mrs. Lyle said placidly that servants of a kind were easily found in Montoak.

"Ah, of a kind! But highly trained domestic servants —where are they?"

Nobody could tell her. From the difficulty of getting servants, she went on to point out the difficulties of travelling in the style to which she had been accustomed to travel in her youth.

"Beautiful staterooms on comfortable liners, trains that ran on time, sleepers you could really sleep in. Porters. Am I expected to act as my own porter?"

"Luggage on wheels?" suggested Ward.

"Thank you. I am *not* going about like a peasant pushing a barrow."

"You could stay at home, as Mrs. Lyle does. You'd have to put her on wheels to move her. If everybody's finished, how about going out and looking round the garden?"

They went outside. It was hardly a garden, but nature, left to itself, had not done badly. Those who liked neat paths and weeded flowerbeds would have been disappointed, but there were wild flowers and golden gorse, and the sunshine, the soft breeze, and the scent of the pines combined to distract the Viscountess from her complaints. Unfortunately, after a time the sun disappeared, the breeze turned to chilly gusts, and the company made their way indoors again. Ward made an attempt to lead the Viscountess to his car, but she was not ready to leave.

"I'd like to go and look at the picture gallery," she said. "I haven't been into it for years."

Ward led them through the empty rooms and down wide corridors covered with faded carpets to the double door of the gallery that had been added to the manor by an eighteenth century owner. The portraits hanging on the walls were not masterpieces, but they represented with few omissions, the successive generations of Rowallens and, in some cases, their wives and families.

They moved slowly down the line of gradually changing fashions, of full wigs and hooped skirts on to the more modern portraits of gentlemen in stovepipe hats, the last looking not unlike Queen Victoria's husband. The Viscountess gazed at him critically.

"I prefer the earlier generations," she said. "I like all the lace and the fancy trousers. As for this"—she stopped and looked up at the next portrait—"it should never have got in here. Why don't you take it down?"

Ward smiled. The woman in the portrait was young, perhaps not thirty, and had a bold, almost gypsy look. She was dressed in a long loose gown round which was a heavy gold belt studded with jewels

"She doesn't fit in, and that outfit looks absurd," the Viscountess went on. "You should take it down."

"Why?" Ward asked. "She's picturesque. And the portrait was hung long before she decamped."

Mrs. Lyle went a step nearer to study the belt.

"Is it real?" she asked.

"Yes," Ward said. "Her husband, the ninth baronet, gave it to her."

"Which he had no right whatsoever to do," pointed out the Viscountess. "It was part of the collection of family jewels. In fact, it was more valuable than all the rest of the collection. And she took it with her?"

"You'd hardly expect her to leave it behind, would you?" Ward asked.

"I wish he'd caught her." The Viscountess turned away. "My father always said she ruined your family."

"After her, the deluge. Yes, I suppose that's true," Ward said.

They filed out of the gallery and Ward drove the Viscountess back to the Plesseys and then made his way to Mrs. Lyle's house. He found her trying to clear up for Philippa the references to the woman of the portrait.

90

"You've always known that sordid history," he told Philippa. "You've seen that portrait dozens of times."

"You never said the belt was real. What happened to it?"

"She had a sound sense of value. It was worth a fortune, so it was the thing she chose to take with her when she ran away."

"What did the Viscountess mean by catching her? Who went after her?"

"The ninth baronet went after her. Are you really interested in her?"

"Yes. Go on."

"There's nowhere to go on to. That was the end."

"Then begin at the beginning."

"Well, it's . . . what are you doing in the kitchen?"

"Come and see. Making a cheese soufflé for my dinner."

"Go easy with the salt. Remember my blood pressure."

"*My* dinner. Go on about the ninth baronet."

"I've had other forebears whose stories were much more . . . "

"Never mind about them. When did he give her the belt?"

"When he was wooing her. She was a well known actress and she was being pursued by a continental princeling. The belt was to tip the scales."

"And it did?"

"Yes."

"He must have known, before their marriage, what kind of woman she was. So why trust her with the most valuable asset the family possessed?"

"He was a lonely widower. His grown-up sons were on the point of marrying, and he was going to be left alone. She was young and beautiful."

"How long did she stay with him before absconding with the jewelled belt?"

"A year."

"Did she run away alone?"

"She went off with a Spaniard called Carlos, who she claimed was her cousin. Do you need all those eggs for a soufflé?"

"Yes. I wish you could tell a story without having to have all the details dragged out of you. She stayed at the Manor for a year?"

"Yes. It must have seemed a long year to her—he seems to have been what they used to call a dull dog. This cousin Carlos had been in London, and came to the Manor on a visit. During his visit, the elder son of the house married, and there was a celebration party at the Manor—great occasion, hundreds of guests. The rest was just pure chance—or, if you like, bad luck for the absconding wife."

"Why?"

"Because she arranged to meet Carlos down on the Ridge—at the point where the Plesseys' house was built later. There was a stream which petered out there—giving just enough water to enable some shrubs to grow. They didn't grow very thickly, and the ninth baronet, chancing to look out of a window, saw his wife with Carlos."

"And went after them?"

"I'm sorry to say that his first concern was to discover whether she had taken the belt with her. She had. Only then did he fling on a cloak and go out. His younger son wanted to go with him, but the old man didn't want anyone to suspect what was going on, so he told him to stay behind. And that was the last time he saw his father alive."

"Why?"

"The old man didn't return. When, about midnight,

they instituted a search, they found that the bridge at the foot of the Manor hill had collapsed and he had fallen into the stream and drowned.''

"And she got away?''

"She certainly didn't come back.''

"So the belt went too?''

"Yes.''

"Well, it was hers,'' said Philippa. "He gave it to her.''

"He did, but as it was the major part of the family so-to-speak treasure, you'd expect her to . . . ''

"No, I wouldn't,'' said Philippa. "She simply took what was hers.''

The argument was checked by a call from the front door. Mrs. Lyle went out and met Mrs. Beetham entering the hall.

"I know you're going to press me to make a longer stay,'' she said, advancing uninvited to the drawing room. She nodded to Ward and Philippa and punched the cushions of one of the chairs preparatory to sitting down and making herself at home. "We've had a terrible day, Harold and I. Yes, thank you, just a little if it's a dry sherry. We've been in Canterbury since morning, seeing house agents. I'm rather glad I wasn't here to meet the Viscountess—I heard she was foisted on you for tea, Ward. Did she have any comment to make on Laura and Selma's move? I suppose not. Much she cares about them. She pretends she didn't sell up after their father died until the girls had decided to live elsewhere—but it's quite well known that she simply announced her intention of selling, and left them to find somewhere else to live. And all that money she's living so luxuriously on—she's only entitled to half the income, but what hope have mousey creatures like poor Laura and Selma of standing up to a woman like that? No news of any house for them—I just dropped in to ask. But at last, at *last* the school authorities are doing something about it, because they now realise that if those two can't get somewhere fairly near, they'll have to give up the nursery school—and you know the uproar that would cause among the mothers." She looked hopefully at her empty glass. Ward held the sherry bottle up to the light, shook his head regretfully and poured her out a thimbleful. He then said he had to see somebody, and took his leave.

"I didn't come here to talk about the Viscountess," Mrs. Beetham went on. "I wanted you to be the first to know that we've made up our minds—at last. We're selling."

There was a pause. Her listeners looked at her expectantly.

"Leaving Montoak?" Mrs. Lyle asked at last.

"Yes. Not a sudden decision, as you well know. And not an easy one, either. When we built this house, we planned to stay in it. We never contemplated having to give it up and settle ourselves somewhere else at our age. But live next door to a car park and surrounded by trippers, I will *not*."

After another pause, Mrs. Lyle said that they would be missed.

"Yes, I think we will," Mrs. Beetham conceded with complacency. "We've pulled our weight all the time we've lived here. We were the first to build on the Ridge, and although—I say this in confidence—it never became quite the shall-we-say intimate society Harold and I had hoped it would, we never had the slightest unpleasantness with any of our neighbours. Yes, I don't think it's claiming too much to say that we shall be missed."

"When . . . " Mrs. Lyle began.

"When shall we go? It depends. We're not getting nearly as much for the house as we'd hoped to, but the

94

agent we finally chose told us that there would be no difficulty in finding a buyer. He had, in fact, one in mind—people who from the sound of them would be at home here. But when he offered them the house, they said it would be too large for them. They're a couple from London, over middle age. They're called MacRobert. No children. Harold and I have never found it too large; we built it, of course, for our own needs—we both dislike cramped quarters."

"Did the deal fall through?"

"Not entirely. They've gone back to London to think it over."

"When you sell, where will you go?"

"We shan't live in a house again. We've decided that we're too old to spread out and undertake the work of keeping a garden going. We've got our eyes on a nice roomy flat within a stone's throw of Harrods: porter, lift, rubbish down a chute and laundry picked up and returned, all that kind of thing. All we have to wait for is the MacRoberts' decision. I have a feeling they may take it. They're extremely well off; I feel rather cheated that they'll get the house for so much less than it's worth."

"We'll miss you," Mrs. Lyle said. "There's been so little change here on the Ridge. I've got used to everybody."

"We shall come and visit you from time to time," Mrs. Beetham said. "We shan't lose touch." She rose. "I'd rather you said nothing about it until things are more definite."

"Of course not."

"Don't get up. I can see myself out."

Philippa however, saw her to the door. Before leaving, Mrs. Beetham had something more to say.

"I'm going to make a confession, Philippa. Harold and I were very glad to hear of your engagement, and do you know why? Not only because you had found a suitable husband. We had been just a little worried that when you came back, if you came back unattached, you might become involved with Ward Rowallen. I'm a great believer in propinquity, and now that he appears to have settled down here, you might—who knows?—have succumbed to this irresistible attraction I'm told he exercises but which I have never seen the slightest sign of. Harold and I think it wouldn't have done at all, so we were more than happy to know that you were, let us say, in no danger. There, I've told you. We always interested ourselves in your welfare, as you know. Now I'll say goodbye. I shall let your mother know when we have news about the house."

Philippa returned to the drawing room and stood looking down thoughtfully at her mother.

"I wish I had your nature," she said.

"Why?"

"Because I'd be able to take people as they came—as you do. Don't you ever get upsurges of loathing for people like the Beethams?"

"I don't think so. Perhaps that's one thing I learned from a roving existence—that you have to accept people as they are. Letting them irritate you is silly."

"It's not silly, it's natural. Don't tell me you ever liked the Beethams, him or her."

"Liked? No."

"Or Denise's father or his frightful second wife?"

"No. But neighbours are neighbours whether you like them or not, and it's no use wasting time trying to change them."

"Did you feel the same way when you were young?"

"As far as I remember." She smiled. "I grew up with much more discipline than I ever subjected you to. I had very little to say in anything that went on. My parents

96

had their career and they took me along with them. I was like . . . ''

" . . . the comet's tail?''

"Yes. I certainly had no voice in any decision and my opinion was never asked about any matter, or about any of the people we came across in our travels. In a way, I suppose it was good training.''

"For what?''

"For learning to be tolerant. Sometimes I think I'm too self absorbed, too detached—but it's saved me from . . . embroilment.''

Philippa had moved to the kitchen. Standing at the open door, she was beating egg whites.

"We know some MacRoberts, don't we?'' she asked.

"Perhaps you do. I don't.''

"The name's familiar, but I can't remember . . . perhaps it was a girl at school.''

"Or perhaps someone you came across in Canada?''

"No. It was further back than that. I'll ask Denise tomorrow.''

Denise arrived soon after breakfast. She proved to have no recollection of the MacRoberts. Ward, arriving soon afterwards and giving every sign of settling down for the day, said, when asked, that he had never met anybody of that name.

"Scots, obviously,'' he said. "You must have come across them on the grouse moors. Why have you got them on your mind?''

"I'm just looking for a connection—a tie-up. It's not important.''

"Good. Then I can announce that Denise and Reid and you and I are dining out tonight. You've got the casting vote as to whether we eat Chinese or Indian. I'm Chinese and so is Denise. Reid and Justin are Indian, so it's up to you.''

97

"You didn't say anything about Justin."

"Well, he's in it. It's really his idea. I've been trying to bring the restaurants in this town up a notch or two. I don't expect them to get into the Michelin Guide straight away, but I hoped to make a start. Justin says I'll get nowhere unless I appoint a panel of gastronomic judges and do the thing on a professional basis. So far, I've appointed Justin and myself. Also invited to stand: Mr. Harold Beetham, because after all he once did a tour of the Bordeaux vineyards, and Monsieur Ducroix, newly arrived head of the French section of the Adult Education Centre."

"Is he a culinary expert?" Denise asked.

"I don't know yet. When I went to see him I was a bit taken aback to find him eating the same food they dish out at the snack bar, but I addressed him as a man who, being French, ought to be a gourmet, and I think I put him on his mettle. The only other person I hope to rope in is Lord Basquine. He doesn't belong here, but he drops in now and then to see his cousins the Plesseys, and takes them out to lunch. Five ought to be enough."

"There isn't one woman on the panel," Denise pointed out. "I protest."

"Who would you suggest? Mrs. Springer?"

"Why not? At least one restaurant ought to serve English food perfectly cooked, and that's her speciality. You ought to know. I've watched you getting through her oxtail stews and her Yorkshire puddings—how many helpings did you have of those joints of roast pork with crackling and . . . "

"All right. Mrs. Springer it is. Six judges. Now we go back to our problem for tonight. Indian or Chinese? Bamboo shoots or Bombay duck?"

Philippa opened her mouth to say she had letters to write and would rather stay at home, and closed it again. She certainly had letters which would have to catch tomorrow's post, chief among them being Dudley's. But it would not be true to say that she would rather stay at home than join the party of diners-out. And there would be more to tell Dudley . . .

"Do we try and get a girl for Justin, to make the numbers even?" Ward was asking.

"No. If Sylvie saw him out with another girl, she might stage one of her drama school scenes," said Denise.

Ward looked at her in surprise.

"What has Sylvie to do with it?" he enquired.

"She's after him. Why do you think she volunteered to run Reid's office?"

"Tell me."

"To give her an excuse for being in Montoak and chasing Justin."

"Does he know?"

"He must have some idea. You can't remain exactly unaware of Sylvie, can you?"

"So what's he doing?"

"Pretending he hasn't noticed anything. Which is more than most men would be able to do in the circumstances."

"Couldn't you point out to her, very mildly, that he's very happy leading the life he's leading and, if he marries at all, he'll choose one of that family of cousins that comes over to see him in their turn-of-the-century car. She's wasting her time."

"They're wasting their petrol. Sylvie wants him and I think Sylvie'll get him."

"You mean you'd actually like to see Justin married to Sylvie Springer?"

"*Married*?" Denise said in astonishment.

"*Married*?" echoed Philippa. "Are you crazy?"

"Well, what else?" he demanded.

The two girls stared at him.

99

"Perhaps he's just naive," Denise suggested.

"No. He's putting on his village idiot act."

"Well, as long as they're not thinking of marrying. Imagine those two united," Ward said in wonder. "Chalk and cheese."

"More poetic imagery," Philippa commented. "In my opinion, he could do worse. She's a nice girl under all that haystack hair and Musketeer boots and Eau de Nuit. All the same, we won't ask her to dinner tonight. We'll stay at five."

"Indian or Chinese?"

"Chinese, as long as we don't go to that fake place called the Kung Foo or whatever."

"We'll go to the Mandarin."

"My father did the décor for that one," Denise said.

"He did it extremely well. The pagoda front fetches a lot of customers. Wait till you see it, Philippa," Ward said.

"If you'd gone about this scheme the right way," she told him, "I would already have seen it. It would have been photographed and the photograph would have appeared in the *Montoak Mail* with a write-up. What's the use of a panel? What you need is the press. Everyone in this town reads the *Montoak Mail,* and a deader publication I never read in my life. Who wants to know all about new building sites and plans for drainage and who's going to be the next town councillor? What's needed to get things going is a newspaper that turns a searchlight on what's going on in town. New restaurants, new sports grounds—how much has there been over those? Nothing. They . . . "

"I was coming to that," Ward said.

"Coming to what?"

"The press. If you . . . "

"You hadn't given one moment's thought to the

press. All you've been doing is going round getting free meals in . . . "

"Free!"

"If they aren't free, you'd better warn the panel of judges. No free meals and they'll resign in a body. Who do you know on the staff of the paper?"

"Everybody."

"Then tell them to take time off and study journalism."

"You can tell them yourself. I'll arrange lunch tomorrow for you and Guy Silvering and myself."

"Who's Guy Silvering?"

"An Oxford playmate who turned up a couple of years ago working for the *Montoak Mail*. He calls himself the Features Editor. If he's free, we'll give him an expensive lunch and tell him what to feature."

"Can't I come too?" Denise asked.

"No. We'll give him Philippa undiluted. After lunch I want to take her for a long drive and try to persuade her that she's making a big mistake in forsaking all her old friends."

It was a good lunch, better than the evening's Chinese dinner, but at the outset it was not a cheerful one. Guy Silvering had a tall drooping body, a long drooping face and spirits that matched his appearance. The meal, he admitted, was better than any he had eaten in Montoak; whether this was due to Ward's missionary activities or to the fact that a new chef had been imported from Belgium, he was not prepared to say.

"But *I* made them import the chef." Ward speared a piece of his Sole Florentine and waved it in emphasis. "I'm beginning to get results. But Philippa thinks I ought to have left the restaurants sleeping and prodded you awake. You're not going to pretend, are you, that your paper is a live organ?"

101

Guy eyed his wine glass until it was refilled.

"Success, they used to tell me, was giving people what they wanted," he said when he had wiped his lips. "I didn't believe it until I came to this place and worked on this paper. I gave the people what I felt certain they'd be glad to have: good journalism. I made the paper—my department of the paper—informative and interesting. I tried to turn the myopic orbs of the inhabitants towards matters of less local and more general interest. They responded by cancelling their subscriptions. So I had to get back to what was showing at the cinema, what they could expect to see on their telly screens, and what bargains they could expect at the forthcoming summer sales. I like this wine—has it always been on their list?"

"No. Entirely due to me." Ward ordered another bottle. "Go on about how you nearly ruined the paper."

"Exactly what are you after? It's no use giving me a general idea. I've already got the general idea: you fill me full of food and wine and tell me to fill my column with—well with what?"

"I don't know anything about journalism," Philippa said, "but I go along with Ward when he says that this town has a choice. It either stays the way it was—hopelessly stuck in the mud, dull, a collection of uninteresting shops and houses—but a town which by chance just happens to have turned into a show place for historians. Or it becomes one of those attractive places you find mostly along the south coast—shops which are offshoots of London shops, small, beautifully-set-out places claiming to sell antiques but really offering nothing more than pieces of Victoriana you can give your aunts at Christmas, two or three first class hairdressers and, as Ward says, good restaurants. Unexpected little French-looking cafés which actually put chairs and tables on to the pavement if it's ever warm enough. Travel agents who offer you the world instead of package tours to the Costa Brava. Boutiques. Small libraries which are like friendly clubs, full of daylight and nobody whispering on tiptoe like in this dreary public one. You think the people here don't want any of this. I think they do—anyhow, the women do. Why do people go to Canterbury, or all the way up to the West End? To look for something to wear, mostly, something that didn't go out the year before last.''

"People," pursued Ward, "are beginning to look for property in and round this town. It was once a farming community, but the farmers are now farming beyond the Ridge; the town's purely commercial. There's a lot of money here, and there's going to be more. So what you . . . ''

"O.K., O.K. I'll make you an offer." Guy addressed Philippa. "If you've got any real ideas—not just pipe dreams, but real ideas that I can turn into articles, I'll use them. If the paper goes out of circulation, it won't be my fault, it'll be yours. You'll have to fork out for some more lunches to sweeten my colleagues.''

"Any time you say," promised Ward. "But you'll admit that this town could have a facelift?''

"I'll admit that a lot of money's beginning to come into it. Take that new branch of Boots: it's larger than any branch south of London. The new Sainsbury's is going to take in two blocks. And I suppose you can read the signs when a man like MacRobert plans to open one of his record shops here. There isn't a Lorenz Disco anywhere between Bond Street and Brighton. He . . . ''

"A what?''

Philippa was looking at him with a frown.

"What was that you said?" she asked.

"I said there isn't a Lorenz Disco . . . I suppose you know what the Lorenz Discos are?"

"Of course I know. But what have they got to do with Mr. MacRobert?"

"MacRobert *is* Lorenz. In case you think I've missed out on this too I can inform you that I interviewed MacRobert last week, chiefly to find out whether it was a rumour, or whether he was really opening one of his branches here. He is. I made the point, talking to him, that there aren't all that many youths and maidens here —not enough, that is, to provide him with the number of customers he'll need to make another million out of sales. He said—as you've just both said—that I'm out of touch. He doesn't want youths and maidens. He said that the record-buying age, today, is from twelve to fourteen. God knows where they get the money. I said babysitting and he said blackmail, but get it they do, and when I was talking to my editor, he said the same thing: it's the pre-teenagers who buy the recordings and fill the pop concerts and do the shrieking and the screeching. He also said . . . "

Philippa was not listening. She had been seeking a connection, and Guy Silvering had provided it—but there was something else, another missing piece, a final thread to knot. Perhaps her mother could . . .

It was late before she could ask her. It was after midnight when, having driven round the countryside with Ward and ended by dining with him in Canterbury, she refused him a nightcap and sent him home.

Her mother was in her room, but there was a light under the door. Philippa knocked, and was told to enter. Her mother was reading in bed, propped against pillows.

"Nice day?" she enquired.

Philippa sat on the edge of the bed. Yes, she answered, it had been a nice day. They had given Guy Silvering lunch and then they had driven round Montoak looking at shop windows and they had decided that window dressing was another matter to which Ward could give his attention. They had dined in Canterbury. She did not add that not once during the day and the evening had she remembered that somewhere, far, far away, there was a man named Dudley Errol . . .

"I suppose," she asked slowly, "it would be difficult for you to keep Ward away from this house?"

For some moments, her mother seemed too astonished to reply.

"Why would I want to keep him away?" she asked at last. "He's been in and out all his life, all your life. While he was in Montoak, he made this his second home."

"I know."

"Why did you suggest . . . ?"

"I'm finding him rather difficult to cope with, that's all."

"Cope? I don't understand."

"Neither do I. I'm used to his way of talking; half of it is hot air and the other half's a kind of experiment in provocation. I've always taken it as it comes, but . . . I just thought it would be nice if I didn't have to see so much of him while I'm here."

"Do you mean he's being troublesome?"

"In a way. He's taking the line that my engagement is a mistake and should never have happened."

"He's only saying what everyone else is thinking, Philippa. He's not the only one who thought . . . The news came just when people—all your old friends—were preparing to welcome you home. From one letter to the next, you became engaged. Denise came to me to ask what I thought about it. William wondered if your father had in some way influenced you. Ward's only saying what we all felt."

"Then he should stop saying it. I'm tired of thinking up crushing remarks."

"If he ever said anything . . . but I'm sure he wouldn't."

"Anything disloyal or anti-Dudley? It might be easier if he did. He keeps on the fringe. He pretends he's seeing me with newly opened eyes. In between the long arguments to convince me that I belong here, he slips in suggestions that I could use these weeks until Dudley comes to decide whether I want to leave here for ever— or not."

"If you're sure about your feelings for Dudley," her mother said, "nothing, no teasing on Ward's part, should worry you."

"Is that all it is—teasing? The point is, it's impossible to avoid him or evade him—he's free to come to this house whenever he wants to, and to stay as long as he likes. Before I realised what he was doing, he'd got me into his town improvement schemes, and now I feel . . . caught. It's no use asking you to say anything— what could you say? Stop pestering my daughter?"

"Pestering?"

"What else?"

"Ward isn't a man who would dream of . . . "

" . . . trying to break up my engagement? It seems to me exactly what he's doing. I don't know what Dudley's making of it all."

"You've mentioned him to Dudley?"

"How can I avoid mentioning him? Everything I do and everywhere I go—Ward Rowallen, Ward, Ward, Ward. What else is there to write about except the weather?"

There was silence. She had not expected her mother to tender advice. She had listened. She had made a

106

comment or two. But it sufficed. It was all she had ever done or ever would do—but who could ever give advice that anybody else would take? Advice—advice on any subject ranging from what colour lipstick to use, which pair of shoes to buy, up to the larger issues of love and marriage—who wanted advice?

She ended the long silence with a sigh.

"Well, it won't be for much longer. And in the meantime . . . "

In the meantime, she would let things take their course. She had been immune to Ward's attractions in the past; all she had to do, until Dudley's arrival, was keep relations between herself and Ward on the surface, keep his mind and hers on the schemes for improving the town—and do her best to keep the memory of Dudley from slipping away altogether.

"Sleepy?" she asked her mother.

"No."

"I didn't mean to talk about Ward. What I came in for was to ask you something—not anything important, just a sort of connection . . . "

"What is it?"

"It was a long time ago. I told you that the name MacRobert had rung a bell, but I couldn't place him. At lunch today, Guy Silvering said that MacRobert was the man who was the head of Lorenz."

"Those enormous shops that sell records?"

"Yes. He *is* Lorenz. I knew that, but it was so long ago, and I had so little to do with the affair, that I'd forgotten."

"An affair?" Mrs. Lyle closed her book.

"Affair is the wrong word. Do you remember the second job I had?"

"Yes. You wanted more money than you were getting in Canterbury, so you took a job in London at . . . Ah. Lorenz."

107

"Yes. Lorenz. I wasn't working in the shop. I was in the office. I was just one step higher than a stamp licker. Sometimes someone would say 'Take a letter, Miss Lyle,' but usually all I had to do was make the tea and take telephone messages while my superiors were out enjoying morning coffee. But they did give me some filing to do—very dull correspondence, invoices and so on. Until one day I was told to open a new file and put it away in a cabinet marked DEAD."

"Deceased staff?"

"No. Matters which had been for some reason held up to be referred to the big chief—Mr. MacRobert."

"Matters such as . . . ?"

"Anything ranging from discovering a drug pusher on the staff trying to do business, to someone trying to fiddle with the cash payments. This case I was given to file, when it was all over—when it had stopped short of being a real court case—was about a woman who was supposed to be selling records and cassettes, but who for over a year, they found, had been making a packet by letting her friends, and her friends' friends, smuggle in baby tape recorders and make their own recordings. The smugglers paid her one pound per record. Lorenz never found out how much money she'd made, but they could make a rough estimate—and it was impressive. She also took home cassettes and brought them back the next day—having hired them out to be recorded."

"How did the firm find out?"

"I don't know. The file started when she was called into the office and questioned. It was pretty serious, so it had to go to the top: Mr. MacRobert. He came up from his house in Guildford. I didn't see him, and I never saw the woman. It was really all over before I got into the firm. I only remember it because when she was sacked, which was after they'd decided not to take the case to court, she left an address—and the address was here, care of a bank in Montoak. When I came home, I thought I'd do some research and see if I could find out who and where she was, but she was called Mary Miller, and there were four pages of Millers in the phone book and they needn't have had any connection with her. So I lost interest and I probably wouldn't have thought about it ever again if I hadn't heard Mr. MacRobert's name. Do you think he ever knew his ex-employee landed up in Montoak?''

"I don't suppose so.''

"Did you ever know any Millers?''

Her mother hesitated.

"Only one," she said at last.

"A family?''

"No.''

"Then . . . ?''

There was a pause. Then Mrs. Lyle spoke quietly.

"Denise's stepmother," she said, "was called Mary Miller.''

She waited for Philippa to realise the implication of this information. It was some time before she spoke again, and then it was with some hesitation.

"You won't say . . . ''

"Anything to anybody about this? You didn't have to ask.''

"I know you don't as a rule—but to Denise . . . ''

"To Denise least of all. Have you . . . had you any idea there was anything like this in her stepmother's past?''

"There were always rumours while she was running that coffee bar. Nothing definite. The tradespeople weren't paid—I think Denise's father paid her debts when they married. After that, he avoided his old friends and joined her set. It was a good thing Denise left the house and went to live somewhere else—she was

109

better away from them. And now, darling, go to bed and get some sleep. You look tired."

Philippa leaned over and kissed her. "I'll try. But I've got a lot to think about."

5

The following week, the Plesseys were officially informed that their Japanese garden was to be undermined in order to allow the excavators to uncover a further length of Roman pavement. The news, which their friends had felt would shatter the pair, was received by them with philosophical calm—it would not, they told one another and their friends, mean that all the labour of constructing the garden would have been wasted. All they had to do was remove the little bridge, the little pagoda, the borders to the paths, the figures—and all these could be put in place when they moved to another home, another garden.

Where this was to be was not yet certain. The fathers of the Plessey pupils began to work each evening on the demolition, while the mothers went to the school, eager to offer the sisters temporary hospitality.

It became apparent that the pleasure of making a Japanese garden was nothing to the fascination of watching it demolished or dismantled. Groups of spectators gathered to watch the five weighty stones lifted by the perspiring labourers. The seven storied pagoda was dismantled and its parts carefully removed. The stone lanterns, each on a base standing about three feet high, and the arched wooden bridge painted lacquer red with ornamental posts and dragons on top were transferred to a corner of the Roman villa and neatly stacked ready to be reassembled.

A rumour, faint and getting fainter, that the Beethams' house might be sold and divided and the lower flat made available for leasing died when no prospective buyer appeared. Mrs. Beetham assured them that the plan might still be put into execution.

"I'm not saying it was definite," she told the sisters. "But the agent did have great hopes of selling. We shall hate going, but it would be nice to think of you two in those lovely rooms—and it's only from the upstairs windows that the view of the car park is . . . "

"Everything," said Selma sensibly, "depends on the rent. It's not the slightest use asking us to pay a fortune, because we haven't got one, but it would be nice not to have to leave the Ridge."

"*You*'ve never liked the ruins, Mrs. Beetham," Laura said. "Now, *we* have. Devastation, you called it. Well, you can't make omelettes without eggs, can you? That's to say, without breaking eggs. And every one of those people who come here to go over them, I mean of course not the eggs but the ruins, goes away knowing more than when they came about those early Romans. Sometimes, looking down at it all, I can imagine myself transported back in time, turned into a Roman house-wife. Selma, shall we tell Mrs. Beetham about your splendid idea?"

"Of course. Everybody will know about it soon."

"Well, it's this. You know that Selma and I always give a little entertainment at the end of the nursery school terms?"

Mrs. Beetham said yes, she did know, and very successful they were too.

"Well, Selma woke me the other night to tell me . . .

111

she gave me a terrible scare, appearing suddenly in the doorway. It must have been somewhere around four o'clock in the morning."

"I didn't actually wake you, Laura. I just stood there, but the door had creaked when I opened it."

"You were saying . . . " prompted Mrs. Beetham, who never had unlimited time to spare.

"Four o'clock. It may have been just after. The clock in my room isn't reliable. It belonged to my father. My mother didn't want me to have it, but fortunately he had actually mentioned in his will that I was to have it, so I was able to carry it off. People should always be precise when they're making wills, don't you agree?"

"Yes, I do. Weren't you telling me about your entertainments?"

"Were we? I wouldn't be surprised," Laura said. "Once we get on to the dear little school, we can't stop."

"What was this idea you had?"

"It was my idea," said Selma. "Laura and I are writing a little play. You know, of course, that we always have to write our own? Our difficulty is always finding plays that will provide parts for forty-two children. One can, of course, bunch groups of them into a chorus, but they don't enjoy it. A child likes to feel he's having a share in the story. I remember so well at school when Laura wasn't given a part in the play. She didn't want to play the lead, don't think that for a moment . . . "

"Certainly not," said Laura. "I couldn't have done it, even if they'd asked me. All I wanted was a line or two, no more."

"And that's what we give the children," Selma resumed. "So . . . "

"Your idea?" Mrs. Beetham tried in vain to suppress her impatience.

"My idea—do let us know frankly what you think of it—is to get permission to stage the play on the site of the Roman villa. It would be a play about the Romans meeting the new Christians. Nobody seems very sure about the actual date of the villa, but we're not going to worry too much about that. We shall have the good Christians converting the pagan Romans. Costumes will be no difficulty, because we shall use sheets—Laura is very clever with drapery. We can always get plenty of assistance with scenery from the fathers of the pupils—don't you remember that splendid inn they built for our nativity play? We shall make the villa look perhaps as it once looked. The only difficulty is rain."

"Yes, rain," breathed Laura, closing her eyes and picturing a downpour. "Rain would ruin everything."

"I think it's a wonderful idea." Mrs. Beetham was backing away. "I do hope my husband and I won't have gone by then. I shall let you know as soon as I hear any definite news."

No news of any kind, however, came from the agent at Canterbury. The name of MacRobert was heard no more, and the only one who remembered it was Philippa, who had allowed herself to make plans which she now feared would have to be abandoned.

She had had little time, lately, for making plans of any kind. She was doing more and more work for Ward. He arrived every morning with a sheaf of papers which he spread on the breakfast table and invited her to inspect. Besides his cataloguing, he had now appointed the panel of so-called gourmets who were to judge the food in any restaurant which would submit itself to gastronomic tests. He was making drafts of publicity columns with Guy Silvering and bringing them round to Philippa to type. The system whereby un- authorised town dwellers could offer themselves as guides and impart inaccurate information to trusting tourists was to be stopped, and a list of competent cicerones drawn up. Philippa had begun as a listener, then had become an assistant and was now a participant. She spent her days driving round with Ward, attending meetings, taking down minutes, sending out invitations or suggestions or information.

Her letters to Dudley had become easier to write; she now had merely to keep him in touch with the growing sophistication of Montoak. If there was more about Ward than about herself in the letters, it was because nothing, now, seemed to happen without him. She marked on a calendar the days that were left before Dudley's arrival. She got out his letters and put them into chronological order and read them in bed, and tried not to feel dismayed when she woke in the morning to find that she had fallen asleep halfway through, and the closely written papers were lying strewn on the rug beside her bed.

She was happy. Her mother watched her but said nothing. Reid and Denise watched her and decided to say something. They gave her lunch in Reid's above-garage flat and attacked her over the coffee.

"We got you here," Denise said, "to ask you what's going on."

"You ought to know what's going on," Philippa said. "I sent you both a long news sheet about everything that . . . "

"Thank you. We got it, both of us. We read it. Interesting, all of it. But that isn't what I meant, and you know it. We haven't got much time—I've got to be at work in half an hour and Reid's got a job that's taking him all the way to Salisbury. So listen. We don't want to interfere in anything you do, but we don't like what you've been doing lately."

"I've been helping Ward."

114

"Fine. What Reid thinks is that while you've been helping Ward, Ward's been helping himself."

"Helping himself to your time and your interest," Reid went on. "Which both belong to this chap you're engaged to. He's a long way away, and I don't know how much you've told him, but I think you ought to tell him some more."

"I came home for two months. Take off the two weeks that Dudley will be here and that leaves six weeks. Six weeks is a long time to sit around doing nothing. I like helping Ward."

"And nobody denies that you're a big help," Reid continued. "But Denise and I have been comparing the time you help him with work and the time you help him with driving round looking at scenery—scenery a long way away from this town. What did your trip to London, to Brighton, to look at boats at Henley—how much did all that have to do with Montoak?"

"Nothing," Philippa answered. "Did you begin by saying you weren't interfering?"

"I didn't. Denise did. I'm interfering because I know Ward. We all know Ward. He . . . "

"If you think he's said anything or done anything that Dudley would have objected to, you're . . . "

Reid drew his chair nearer and spoke in the tone Laura or Selma would have used to a rather slow pupil.

"The point is, Philippa, Ward doesn't have to do anything. Ward doesn't have to say anything. In all the years I've known him, I've never heard that he's done anything or said anything that any girl, any woman would be able to call encouraging. He just goes on being himself. The big mystery—to me—has always been that there doesn't seem much about himself to account for the effect he has on the opposite sex."

"Ward is . . . "

"Ward is a nice guy. Ward, as far as I know, is a

straight guy. But you and he have been what my Dad calls running in harness these past weeks, and what happens if you suddenly get to thinking he's more your type than this chap who's stuck thousands of miles away waiting to come and collect you?''

There was silence. Philippa stared at the film of coffee at the bottom of her cup. Denise spoke.

"I think Reid's putting it a bit too strongly," she said. "After all, as I pointed out to him, you've been around Ward all your life. If you were going to fall for him, you'd have done it around the time that I fell for him—when we were adolescents. It isn't *that* I'm worried about, I just don't want you to get yourself mixed up in your mind, that's all. And I mean that's all. We've said it and that's all we'll say."

"Except that I think Ward's doing this town facelift a bit too seriously," Reid remarked. "Change is all very well, and God knows the place needed some, but too much is too much. Why is Ward letting in that London hairdresser? The . . . ''

"He isn't. I thought it was a bad idea, so I stopped it," said Philippa. "I went to see Bascombe's manager, and then the two of us had a meeting with the owner, Mrs. Bascombe, and I said that all she had to do if she wanted to keep out competition was to make that stock room into a reception room and use the present reception room for extra basins and driers, and get more staff and dress them in pretty overalls. I suggested hiring Sylvie as a model.''

"You *what*?" Reid demanded.

"They have them in Canada in the international salons—girls who model hairstyles. Sylvie's got the perfect face for it, and Guy said he'd photograph her for free. Did Ward tell you there's a possibility of some of the tradespeople in the town getting loans?''

"He did not. Who's shelling out the loans?''

"The town authorities—once they approve the plans for improvement. It's no use asking some of the less prosperous ones to launch out unless you give them something to launch with."

"Well, I need four new vans. How about putting me up for some of the cash?"

"Never mind the new vans," Denise said. "If Sylvie's going to model hairstyles, who's going to run Reid's office?"

"You are," Philippa told her.

Ward's reactions to a similar conversation were less calm. He chose a moment when he and Philippa, after a picnic lunch, were seated under a tree in the Manor grounds, sheltering from a sun that had become almost too warm.

"I suppose," he told Philippa, "that you, like myself, got the big brother treatment from Reid and Denise?"

"What do you call the big brother treatment?"

"By the big brother treatment I mean interfering in affairs that don't concern them. I'm not surprised at Denise, but I'd have thought Reid would have sized up the situation better than he has done."

Philippa took her time. "I didn't know," she said, "that there was a situation."

"Perhaps you didn't know that there was a situation before they told you there was a situation, but you can hardly brush off what they said without talking it over with me, can you?"

"I don't honestly think there's anything to talk about."

"There's a situation to talk about and, as I see it, it's this: they think I'm seeing too much of you, and they consider that my seeing too much of you is a bad thing. Would you like my views on the subject?"

117

"You're going to give them to me anyway, aren't you?"

"Yes. As follows: I see you as a girl who's engaged to another man. If you were *married* to another man, and I happened to be in love with you—as I am—there'd be no question of anybody worrying about my seeing too much of you. My views on married women are that they belong to somebody else. Having had the chance of choosing a man, and having chosen him, I consider that they should stick to him, at any rate for a time. In marrying, a man presumably hopes to make a home for himself and his family, and I think any woman who takes him on should help him to, shall we say, build his nest. So if a married woman attracts me, I leave it at that. But a girl who's *engaged* is a girl who's still free. She has chosen a man, but she isn't linked to him in what they call the sacred bond of matrimony. There's still an interval during which she can reconsider, and during that interval I see no reason why any other man who wants her shouldn't stand up and say so. Therefore, I state clearly, here and now, that I love you very much. I don't know anything about the man whose ring you're wearing, but he must be aware that in letting you come to England alone, in letting you rejoin your old friends—some at least of whom he must know couldn't fail to be aware of your attractions—he is taking a risk, and he must be prepared to run into trouble."

"The point is, Ward . . . "

"Wait. I haven't finished. You're not a girl who's likely to be swayed by any man who makes love to you. You're . . . "

"All I'm trying to say . . . "

"Give me one moment more. What is loyalty? As I see it, it's what you think you owe this fellow in Canada. I'll go along with you that your loyalty is

118

something that he has to rely upon while he's not there to keep an eye on you. But loyalty means keeping him in mind, and not allowing his interests to be threatened until you are absolutely certain that you have found someone to whom you owe more than loyalty. And that's all I've got to say. I claim the right to make love to you and will cede it only when I know that you are irrevocably bound to this Dudley Errol, and not merely by a gold circlet with a handsome diamond on it. I love you. That's a bald statement, but it's the only one I can make. I would give anything in the world to make you the mistress of that mellow but mouldering mansion on top of the hill. I would like you to be the mother of my children. And to that end, I shall make love to you whenever opportunity offers, and to hell with anyone who objects." He turned her face towards his, and laid a gentle kiss on her lips. "Have you been listening?" he asked.

"Can't I make a few points of my own?" she asked.

"No. Your attitude will come out very clearly in your response to my efforts to get you to fall in love with me. You're near it—God knows you're near it—but you're not there yet. But time is still on my side. Now do you want to say anything?"

There were tears in her eyes. She shook her head.

"Are you quite sure you don't want to say anything?"

"Don't let's talk any more," she begged.

"We won't talk any more after you've answered two questions. I'd like truthful answers—no hedging, no holding back for this or that qualm, just the simple truth. Ready?"

"I don't feel that . . ."

"First question. If you were given a choice, a free choice, a choice that didn't drag in any personal element—if you could choose between staying in

England, and going back to Canada, which would you choose? Remember what I said—no personal element to enter into it. Which would you choose?"

She spoke slowly, but with decision.

"I'd stay here."

"Second and last question. Since you became engaged, have you ever—in Canada or over here—had any feeling that you had acted too hastily?"

"That's what they call a loaded question, isn't it?"

"Not necessarily. Women—and men too—sometimes make a decision to marry and then regret it. They can regret it for many reasons. A man might feel that he can't really afford a wife and family. A woman might feel that she'd like a few more years of freedom. In your case, as you've admitted that you'd rather live in England, you might regret that you've chosen to marry a Canadian. Do you?"

She did not answer for some time. He waited patiently.

"In a general sense," she said at last, "I wish he could have been an Englishman. But he isn't, so there's no point in talking about regretting anything, is there?"

"Perhaps not. I just wanted to know, that's all."

He gave a sigh, and enfolded her in his arms.

"Philippa Lyle," he said, "I hereby give my love to you. For ever and ever."

She made no attempt to release herself.

"If I'd never gone away," she said, "you wouldn't have . . ."

" . . . seen you with new eyes? If you hadn't gone away, I would have felt exactly as I do now. You've never acknowledged the bond that there is between us. You've never admitted or agreed that once you grew up you and I were closer to one another than to anyone else. We were two apart. Nothing could have prevented our falling in love—nothing. It would have been the first time for us both, and we would have come together because we were growing nearer to one another—until you went away. Why, oh why did you go away, my lovely Philippa? Why did I let you go?"

She could not have answered. His lips were on hers. She was clinging to him, passion welling up and making her tremble.

She freed herself at last. They did not speak. The trees above seemed to her to have spread their branches in benediction. She had forgotten the past and the future. There was only the present.

When at last she spoke, it was in a calm and reasonable tone.

"Hadn't we been discussing loyalties?" she asked.

"We had. I gave you my view."

"I'll give you mine. Loyalty is what I owe to the man I agreed to marry. You and I have been together a good deal, and I've been happy being with you. But I can't go on seeing you day after day if . . . if . . . "

"If I make love to you? Are you issuing an ultimatum?"

"No. I'm just asking you to let things go on the way they are going—seeing each other, but . . . "

" . . . keeping it on a friendly basis."

"Yes. It's not an ultimatum, it's an appeal. Oh Ward, I've been so happy, so happy . . . "

Tears welled up and she wiped them away. He leaned over and kissed her.

"Go on being happy," he said.

"Friends?" she asked shakily.

"If you want it that way, then yes—friends."

When he saw her the next day, he found her manner not friendly, but businesslike. She wasted no words on a greeting.

"Ward," she said, "I've got something to ask you. A favour."

"Granted."

"I'm serious. I've had an idea."

"About what?"

"It's in three parts. Part one: the Beethams want to sell their house."

"So?"

"A man who could afford to buy several Beetham houses, but doesn't want to because he's looking for a smaller place, has seen the house, liked the house, but is apparently on the point of turning down the house. End of part one."

"Part two?"

"The Plesseys must find somewhere to live. They want to go on living on the Ridge. The Beethams' house would be too hopelessly large for them, but there's a rumour that it's to be divided and the lower flat made available for a tenant."

"Part three?"

"We have on the Ridge an architect. If you . . . "

"You needn't spell it out. If you put parts one, two and three together, you have housed the MacRoberts, housed the Plesseys and given Mr. Luton a fat fee. I'm sorry about that last; I hate to see money going into his pockets."

"So do I. But if you put the three parts together to Mr. MacRobert and explained . . . "

"Me?"

"You. You needn't do it in a direct way—that is, you needn't put it to Mr. MacRobert yourself; all I'm asking is that you see the proposition put to him."

"What proposition?".

"That he buys the house and asks Mr. Luton to divide it in two—one half for the MacRoberts and the other half for the Plesseys. Not selling it to them—renting it.''

"I have to fix all that?"

"Yes." She turned to him and spoke urgently. "You do agree, don't you, that it's a good idea?"

"Yes. But . . . "

"You do agree that if you don't do something to make it possible, it won't come off?"

"Yes. But . . . "

"Do you want to sit there doing nothing while the MacRoberts go and find a home somewhere else, and the Plesseys have to give up the nursery school and leave Montoak?"

"No. But . . . "

"There is no question of any but. You can do it. And the way to do it is to bring the parties together."

"Parties?"

"You have, first of all, to meet Mr. MacRobert. You can easily arrange that through Guy Silvering. The three of you meet—Guy has to arrange it—to have a drink and talk about the future of the town, in a general way. Then you learn, during the conversation, that Mr. MacRobert thought of buying a house here, and actually went out to see the one on offer on the Ridge. That gives you an idea. How would it be, you ask Mr. MacRobert, if he considered the idea of buying and then converting, and then renting a small portion, absolutely self contained, to two delightful ladies, Honourables no less, about to be rendered homeless?"

"I had no idea you were so preoccupied with the future of the two delightful ladies."

"Well, I am, and so should you be, too. Nobody thinks more of you than those two do. Half their time is spent trying to think of things they can do to please you. They think you're some kind of—of . . . "

"Demigod?"

123

"They love you. And what have you ever done for them?"

"Want a list?"

"It wouldn't be a long list if you left out the times you only helped them because it didn't interfere with anything else you were doing. Do you want to see them in the Beethams' house, or not?"

"I want to see them in the MacRoberts' house."

"I'm trying to tell you how it can be done. This idea I've got is a—workable idea. It's *neat*. All you have to do is act as a sort of liaison. Will you do it?"

He kept his eyes on her for some time. There was surprise in his gaze, and then speculation.

"What's behind all this?" he asked at last.

"What's behind all what?"

"Don't dodge. After parts one, two and three there should be part four, which touches on the reason for your fervour."

"Let's just say that I don't often get an idea like this, and when I do, I get excited. Will you arrange that meeting? It ought to be here at the Manor. I don't mean the meeting between you and Guy and MacRobert, I mean a later one when you bring the MacRoberts and the Plesseys together. And when you do that, if Mr. MacRobert has agreed to your recommending an architect, you can ask Mr. Luton to drop in. A nice party; Mr. and Mrs. MacRobert, the Plesseys, Guy, Mr. and Mrs. Luton."

The speculation in his eyes turned to suspicion.

"Look, let's see your hand. You've forgotten how long I've known you. You've got something in mind that you haven't spilled yet. What is it?"

"Will you do it and stop asking questions?"

"No. If you'd suggested my asking Luton to drop in, that's one thing. To go as far as to ask me to include his wife . . . my God, the very idea! What's behind all this?"

124

"Have I ever asked you a favour before?"

"Yes. Lifts to and from town, commissions . . . "

"A real favour. I haven't, ever. Instead of wasting time looking for hidden motives, just look forward and imagine the thing done, and done successfully."

"Do I have to ask the house agent, too?"

"No. We don't want to give Mr. MacRobert the idea that he's being . . . "

". . . pressurised. When do I have to start rounding up the cast?"

"Tomorrow. If you leave it any later, Mr. MacRobert will have gone and the whole plan will collapse."

"You admit it's a plan?"

"It's an idea. Please, Ward. Yes or no?"

He sighed.

"Yes. All right."

6

The first opportunity that the residents of the Ridge had had to study Mr. MacRobert was on the day of Ward's party. He proved to be of middle height, thin, grey haired, and would have been called nondescript if it had not been for his jutting jaw and keen, watchful grey eyes. His manner was unassuming, but there was at the same time something about him that kept people aware that he was a rich and successful man. His wife, on the other hand, was short, stout and homely and gave the impression that she was worrying about something she had left boiling on the stove. She found nothing to say to any of the people to whom she was introduced until Ward led her up to Mrs. Lyle who, she learned after a time, had been—like herself—the victim of men who refused to stay in one place.

"But you had to keep going?" she enquired in an accent which had a strong Scottish flavour. "I mean to say, you couldn't refuse to go, could you?"

"I did refuse in the end. I'd had enough. I loved our house here and I didn't see any reason for giving it up and going all the way to Canada."

"So what did you do?"

"I stayed here."

"But not him?"

"No. He went. I was quite prepared to act as a sort of base camp and let him go exploring whenever he felt like it, but what he wanted was a complete change."

"Just like *him*." Mrs. MacRobert jerked her chin in the direction of her husband, who was in a group that included Ward. "I never get time to settle. I never get to know my neighbours, nothing like that. Just get the furniture into place and my kitchen the way I like it, and then we're packing up again. Now he's talking about buying this big house here."

"I hope he does. I hope you'll be able to stay in it for ever, as I plan to stay in mine."

"What do you think to tenants living in the same house? Could you put up with that?"

"If they were the Plesseys, or people like them, I'd be very happy to have them. But you'd be entirely separate, surely? Separate entrance, separate garden, separate garages?"

"That's what they're planning, yes."

There was a pause—not awkward, but friendly.

"Do you have much influence over . . . " began Mrs. Lyle.

126

"You mean, do I have any say before he signs all the papers? Yes, I do. He wouldn't sign if I said I didn't like the place."

"And do you?"

"Yes. I like a solid house, and this one's solid enough. And I like the neighbourhood."

"And you'll like the neighbours."

They studied one another. Mrs. Lyle wished she had the courage to urge the other woman to throw her weight on the side of purchasing. It would have made a notable difference to the outcome.

"They said there was an architect coming, but I don't think he's turned up," remarked Mrs. MacRobert.

"He was invited," Mrs. Lyle told her. "There's still time for him to . . ."

"Not very keen on the job, from the looks of it. If he wants it, he ought to show some interest. Sometimes they're like that, though, folk who go after a job—they like you to think they've several more up their sleeve. Well, if my husband does buy, and if we need an architect, I daresay there are plenty more where this one comes from. I don't know what he looks like—if he comes, you might point him out. He lives on this estate, doesn't he?"

"Yes. He lives next door to me."

"You won't be far off, if we come here. I'll be glad to know that. You look to me like a body I could get along with. Do you go out much?"

"I never leave my house if I can help it."

Mrs. MacRobert brightened visibly.

"You don't?"

"No. As I told you, I did too much moving around when I was young, so now I stay at home. This party was rather special, so I had to come."

"You'll be the mother of the girl who's getting married and going away to Canada?"

127

"Yes."

"I suppose you'll miss her. Or have you got more children at home?"

"No. She's the only one. But I'm happy on my own."

"Me too. Good thing I am, with a husband who's more out than in. We've got no family. There's only him and me."

A tray of drinks was brought round by Chester. Mrs. Lyle took a glass of sherry; Mrs. MacRobert waved the tray away.

"I'm teetotal," she said. "If you've got a glass of water with a squeeze of lemon in it . . . "

"Certainly, Madam. Ice?"

"No, no ice. Just natural water and real fruit—nothing out of a bottle. If you can't get a nice hot cup of tea," she went on to Mrs. Lyle, "then a squeeze of lemon's the next best. Here's my husband coming with Sir Edward. That architect chap—he didn't come?" she asked them.

"No. Don't worry about the architect," her husband said. "What I'd like from you is what you think of this house we've looked at."

She looked at him with her head on one side.

"You mean if I say No, it's No?"

He nodded.

"That's what I mean. Have I ever put you into any house you didn't like?"

"No. I'll give you credit for that, at any rate."

"Do you like this one?"

"Yes. I do."

"Then we can go ahead?"

"We can."

"And we divide it into two, and let the lower half?"

"Yes. You'll offer it to those two ladies?"

"Yes."

"Then all right."

He turned to Ward.

"It's a deal," he said.

This matter concluded, he turned his mind to another. He addressed Ward.

"That young chap standing over there near the window—forget his name," he said. "Chap with the ginger hair and bat's ears. Golding, or something of that kind."

"His name is Silvering. Guy Silvering." Ward spoke with an edge to his tone. "He works on the . . . "

"Yes, I know what he does. I want a word with him. Fetch him."

There was a slight pause. Mr. MacRobert had not moved, and was obviously waiting for Ward to conduct Guy Silvering to his side. Ward, unwilling to obey an order so peremptory, was on the point of offering to take Mahomet to the mountain when Guy turned and met his eye. In response to Ward's signal, he came across the room and joined him. Mr. MacRobert spoke without preamble.

"I suppose you know who I am, and I suppose you know I've bought a house here."

"I knew," Guy began, "that you were perhaps . . . "

"Well, there's no perhaps. I've got a house here, and that means I'll be spending a good deal of time in this place. And that means I've got to find myself something to do. I've never done anything in the journalistic line, but I've decided to make a start by putting in a bid for this local paper. Who's the owner?"

Guy stared at him blankly.

"The owner? You mean . . . who owns the *Montoak Mail*?"

"That's what I said. I can't make it any plainer, can I?"

"You . . . you're thinking of making a bid for the . . . "

"Now look here." Mrs. MacRobert addressed her husband firmly. "You don't know the very first thing about newspapers, and you don't even know whether this one's for sale, and it's daft to think you can . . . "

"The owner," broke in Ward, "is called Walters. As well as being the owner of the paper, he's its editor. If you want to meet him, Guy can arrange it."

Mr. MacRobert turned to Guy.

"What like of man is he?" he enquired. "How much interest does he take in his paper?"

"He . . . well, he . . . I mean to say . . . " Guy stuttered.

Ward came to the rescue.

"Mr. Walters," he told Mr. MacRobert, "is in his late seventies, and suffers a good deal from gout, which prevents him from going to the newspaper offices as often as he used to."

"Which is doubtless a good thing," Mr. MacRobert said bluntly. "If he's been staying away, it might account for the improvement there's been lately in the paper. It was a poor sort of rag when I first looked at it. Lately, it's taken a turn for the better. Where can I get hold of this owner-editor?"

Guy, pulling himself together, said that Mr. Walters lived on the outskirts of town and had not been in the office for the past two weeks.

"Then I'll go and see him where he lives," said Mr. MacRobert. "I'll drop into the office first and take a look round."

He gave a nod to his wife, and she apparently interpreted this as a summons. Together they took their leave and, accompanied by Ward, made their way out.

Guy awaited Ward's return, and looked at him with a dazed expression.

"Did that"— he jerked his head in the direction the MacRoberts had taken—"mean anything?"

130

Ward frowned.

"I didn't like his approach," he began, "but . . . "

"Never mind the approach. Was he talking seriously, or just talking?"

"I think he certainly wants to buy the paper."

"And then what? Run it?"

"That's the impression I got."

"That's the impression I got, too. How do you think he'll go about it? Is he going to start by sacking all the existing staff, and putting in a new lot?"

"If he'd intended to do that, he wouldn't have called you over and talked to you as he did. Or at least, I don't think so."

"He's spoiled my evening. I was enjoying myself. Now I'm feeling like that fellow who had an axe hanging over his head."

"A sword."

"Same thing when it comes to giving a junior reporter a chop."

"He might promote you."

"And he might not. Could I have another drink?"

Ward brought him one. The guests were leaving. When they had gone, and only Philippa and her mother remained, Ward told Philippa of Mr. MacRobert's plan to buy the *Montoak Mail.* She frowned anxiously.

"That doesn't mean he'll dismiss the present staff, does it?"

"Haven't you ever heard of unions?" Ward asked her. "That's what MacRobert'll have to deal with. All the same, Guy's going to have a few wakeful nights. Perhaps it's just as well Mr. Luton didn't turn up. The architect who gets the job of dividing the house will have his work cut out; MacRobert has his own ideas of what's to be done, and he'll see that the architect does it. I wouldn't like to work for him."

"His wife is nice," Mrs. Lyle said. "I like her. I think

131

she'll like living here. They've got no family—and I think she'll end by adopting Laura and Selma."

"Now that you've really come out, why don't you make a night of it and come out to dinner?" he suggested.

"No, thank you, Ward. I've enjoyed myself, but . . . I'm longing to get home."

He looked enquiringly at Philippa. After a moment, she nodded.

"You mean you'll come?" he asked.

"Yes."

She did not want to go home. She did not want to spend the evening wondering whether the plan, the party, was going to have any effect on the future of Mr. and Mrs. Luton. They had not come. Significant, but not entirely reassuring. He might have stayed away because he might not have cared to accept a commission from Mr. MacRobert, known for driving a hard bargain. His wife may have felt that to leave the house in which she had—in Reid's words—dug herself in, going away from her friends in town might be too high a price to pay for ensuring that she did not meet her former employer. Nothing was certain.

"Do you want to change before you go?" Ward asked her.

"No. This is my party dress, hadn't you noticed?"

"Any particular restaurant in mind?"

"Yes, Chinese."

He looked at her speculatively. "Is that because you're trying to work out a puzzle?" he asked her.

"No."

"We'll go in my car. I'll bring it round."

They dropped Mrs. Lyle at her house, and were driving past the Lutons' when the door opened and Mr. Luton appeared on the doorstep. He signalled to them to stop. Ward brought the car to a halt, and Mr. Luton

132

came slowly down the path towards them. He looked pale, and his manner had none of its usual confidence. He nodded to Philippa, and addressed Ward.

"I'm sorry I didn't show up at the party," he said.

"That's all right."

"I meant to go. I got ready to go. I felt it was imperative for me to meet MacRobert. There were rumours of rebuilding, and I thought there might be a job in it for me. But"—he paused and stared for some moments into the distance—"as a matter of fact something came up which has given me a bit of a knock."

"Then why not come back to the Manor and talk, instead of standing in the road?"

"I . . . Yes, I will, if I may."

Philippa made room for him. Ward turned and drove back up the hill, and the three entered the house.

"Sit down, I'll get you a drink," said Ward.

Glass in hand, Mr. Luton began to speak.

"This afternoon," he said, "my wife went to see my doctor. She said she thought I'd been looking off colour for some time—I don't know why, because I've felt all right. But she had a talk with the doctor, and when she came back, she said he'd told her that I'd got to get out of this country—this climate. So . . . " He paused and drained his glass and spoke with an effort, "We're leaving."

"Where will you go?" Ward asked.

"God knows. Somewhere in the south, I suppose. One of those Latin countries I've always avoided. I don't like heat and I don't like patios and piazzas and lying around under a sun umbrella on beaches crowded with half naked women. I want to stay here. I've never been part of the Ridge social scene, but I like the house I built, and I would have liked to stay in it. But my wife said it would be stupid—and dangerous—to ignore the doctor's orders, so we're going. And then Denise will move into the house with her cockney lover, and have a family of cockney Springers."

"Reid's all right," Ward said.

"If you say so. But apart from being all right, he's devoid of any acceptable social background, he's totally lacking in elementary good manners, and he's entirely content to remain who and what he is. He won't change. It's Denise who'll have to do the adapting. It's that, the fact that he's without social ambition, without any desire to try to measure up to Denise's social level, that made me set my face against their association. But she'll marry him, or move into the house with him, and there's nothing I can do to stop her."

Philippa spoke for the first time.

"You said your wife had seen your doctor. Shouldn't you have gone to see him yourself?"

"Why? I've paid him regular visits for years. There's nothing he doesn't know about my state of health. My wife went this afternoon because she was worried, and wanted to ask him whether I should really go on living in England—and the answer was no."

He sighed, put down his glass, shook his head to Ward's offer of refilling it, and walked slowly to the door.

"I've left a telephone message at Reid Springer's office, asking Denise to come and see me. Not at the house. I'll tell her the news at a pub in town."

He refused Ward's offer of a lift down the hill.

"No, thanks—I'd like to be alone for a while, thinking this over."

They drove away, leaving him standing outside the manor. Ward spoke in a puzzled tone.

"Funny, wouldn't you say?" he asked. "Not funny—I mean fishy."

"Because he didn't talk to the doctor himself?"

134

"Yes. Why would a man make a momentous decision of this kind simply because his wife and his doctor got together and . . . You're not listening."

"Sorry. I was thinking about what he said about Reid. I suppose it's true."

"Of course it's true. And it's true that there are rocks ahead for Denise. She won't try to change him because she likes him the way he is. But she might not want her children to talk like Eliza Doolittle did before she ran into Professor Higgins, so she'll have to decide whether to let them grow up like their father, or like her. But that's her problem. Mine is more pressing—where to park when we get to the Chinese restaurant."

"Why, when you were reorganising the town, didn't you plan more car parks?" Philippa asked him.

"Did I know—did you or anybody else know—that our panel of so-called food experts were going to make the restaurants so popular? Did you or I or anybody else guess that the people of Montoak would begin to dine out? Did we foresee that people would flock in for miles around to occupy tables at the Montoak restaurants? Did we?"

"No."

"So that's why we're short of car parks. But don't worry—I've got the matter in hand."

"Why don't we skip the Chinese restaurant and go and have a meal at that new pub called the Squirrel?"

"Sandwiches for dinner? Thank you, no."

"Not sandwiches. They serve slices of wonderful pies, and hot fat sausages and lovely bits of things on skewers."

"At the Squirrel?" Ward asked in astonishment. "You must have got it wrong. It's a wooden shack that probably dishes out pale ham plastered between plastic slices of bread."

She spoke in exasperation.

"If you appoint a committee, why don't you keep track of what they're doing?"

"It wasn't my idea to choose a panel of food experts. It was Justin Armitage's idea."

"It was his idea, but you did the appointing. Only you didn't do enough follow-up. Mr. Beetham's done wonders at all the restaurants, persuading them to improve their wine lists. Lord Basquine made a round of all the restaurants, taking large parties with him. It was Mrs. Springer who thought of making the pubs serve good food. She makes the pies for the Squirrel."

"Mrs. Springer does?"

"Yes. And there's a large car park there. But you've passed it. You should have turned left at . . . "

She stopped. Ward had done a U-turn. They were on their way to sample Mrs. Springer's pies.

Arriving at the Squirrel, they found Guy Silvering seated at the bar, drooping over a half finished drink, his expression melancholy, his whole bearing a picture of despair.

"Anything wrong?" Ward asked him.

Guy raised a gloomy countenance.

"Nothing's wrong. Nothing at all. It's just that I think my whole future is in ruins."

Ward and Philippa seated themselves on either side of him.

"MacRobert proposed buying the paper," said Ward. "Your future will merely be under a new chief, that's all."

"What he's going to do," Guy said, "is make a clean sweep of the old hands."

"Do you call yourself an old hand? You've only worked on the paper for . . . "

"It doesn't matter how long I've worked on the paper. Once the sale goes through—and it will—that

MacRobert has only to give one glance at old Walters to know he's dealing with a shell, a husk, a has-been. He'll offer him half what the paper's worth, and Walters will pick up his pen and sign, and the whole thing will be over and done with. After that, dismissals and redundancies—in short, the sack for all of us.''

"Want to bet on it?" Ward asked.

"No. It's all very well for you to take a chirpy view—you've at least got a roof over your head. What have I got? A room overlooking the back of the Chinese restaurant."

"Don't kill off your chickens before they're hatched. Why not finish your drink, and then invite us to share a bite with you?"

"All my money will be needed to keep me during an indefinite period of unemployment."

"Then Philippa'll treat us. Pies, sausages—come over here and we'll get a table."

Reluctantly Guy joined them, but his conversation did not cover any fresh themes.

"The point is," he said, as they waited for their food to be served, "that in a case like this, union or no union, every member of the staff gets thrown into the mincer regardless of his or her value to the paper. I don't want to blow my own trumpet, but you know as well as I do that I'm the sole hope the *Montoak Mail* has of getting into the twentieth century. But who'll tell old MacRobert that? Nobody. Certainly not old Walters. He didn't like new ideas, especially mine."

Generous slices of pie flanked by succulent looking sausages were being placed before them. From the plates rose an odour so tempting that Guy forgot his worries and began to eat. With second helpings on order, gloom vanished and the spirits of all three rose. Ward was in one of his lightest moods, and Philippa found herself reflecting that it was wonderful to laugh again—laugh as he and she had laughed in their teens. She knew it would be wrong to say that Dudley had no sense of humour, but it was of a heavy kind, entirely removed from Ward's ability to amuse her with old memories, odd happenings in the passing scene, trifles that struck both of them as laughter-provoking. And she knew that under Ward's light manner there was a serious vein, a steadiness that made her feel as secure as she had felt with Dudley. This was an evening on which she could forget problems, forget the need to make difficult decisions. This was an evening for enjoyment.

On the following morning, Ward made his usual visit to Mrs. Lyle's house to pick up Philippa. He found her alone—Mrs. Lyle was upstairs in her workroom. Ward had not been there long when one of Reid Springer's vans stopped at the gate. Denise was at the wheel. She got out, came into the drawing room, and spoke in an excited voice.

"I've got news," she said. "You'll never believe it, never."

"Sit down and calm down," Philippa advised her. "I'll make you some coffee."

"This news won't wait. All right, thank you, coffee if it's not a bother. But I've got to tell you—it's no use asking you to guess, because it's so fantastic that I don't even know where to begin."

"Begin by taking a long deep breath," said Ward. "Then you can give us your information clearly."

"But you'll never believe it. I can't even believe it myself. It's so fantastic that I almost believe I've dreamt it. And it's so unexpected that . . . ."

"Facts only, please," Ward said. "You can put in the fancy bits afterwards."

"But I just can't . . . "

"If you say you can't believe it once more," Ward

138

said, "you can go away and leave Philippa and myself to plan our day. Now, begin at the beginning."

"The beginning . . . my father and stepmother were invited to your party, weren't they?"

"They were," Ward said, "but they didn't come."

"That's right. They didn't go because . . . "

" . . . because your stepmother thought your father had been looking out of sorts for some time, and went to see his doctor, and the doctor advised a change of climate."

Denise looked at him indignantly.

"If you knew already," she said, "why didn't you say so?"

"We were waiting for you to say so," Ward told her. "Congratulations on getting your house back."

She went up to him and threw her arms impulsively round his neck. "Isn't it wonderful?" she said.

Ward freed himself, and led her to the door. Philippa halted him.

"Her coffee," she said.

Denise sat down, drank half of it, but was too excited to drink the rest. Then she rose to go.

"We're all going to be neighbours," she said happily.

"Not all of us," Ward said.

7

In the evening, when everybody had gone away and the site was empty, Laura and Selma were in the habit of going down to inspect the slowly emerging pavement. The earth that had been lifted and sifted during the day was put aside to be removed the next day. The ground, cut away from the garden, now resembled a kind of quarry, and round this the sisters stepped carefully, making a leisurely survey. On the evening of the party at the Manor, they found dusk coming on before they realised it.

"That's all, Laura," Selma commanded. "Come inside. It's time to make supper."

"I'm not really hungry—are you? I ate things at the party."

"You'll be hungry by the time supper's ready. Come along now."

But Laura lingered, stooping to look more closely at the colours of the pavement.

"I wish I could imagine that hundreds and hundreds of years have gone by since this was made," she said. "At school, when they talked about thousands of years I—Oh!" She slipped, recovered her balance and then slid slowly down a mound of earth, coming to rest with her feet buried in rubble.

"Your *shoes*!" Selma said reproachfully. "I told you and *told* you, Laura, not to come down here without putting on gardening boots."

"I thought it was only going to be for a moment or two."

"Give me your hand—I'll pull you up."

Laura put out a hand and then drew it back. She was stooping once more, this time to pick up a small object from the mud. She held it up for her sister's inspection.

"Look, Selma—isn't that pretty?"

"Will you please step out of that mud? It's not only dirty, it's also damp. You'll catch a chill."

"What do you think it is?" Laura handed it up for inspection. "It's not a bead and it's not a button. If

140

you asked me, I'd say it was some . . . could it be a jewel of some kind?"

Selma was turning it over in her hand, shaking the soil off. "Jewel? Don't be silly, Laura. What would jewels be doing down there?"

"They found lots of things when they were digging up the . . . "

"Of course they did. Fragments of pottery, coins, small articles of household use—things like that. Things that had got broken when the people lived in the villa, things they left behind when they went away. Who would leave jewels behind?"

Laura was bending down and scraping in the soil.

"More—look. Four, five, six . . . " She reached up and dropped the objects into Selma's hand, and then bent down to peer once more at the ground. "And, look, Selma, a bit of chain. Could it be . . . it *looks* like gold."

"Now you're really being absurd, Laura. There's no buried treasure here, you know. Look at your hands—they're filthy!"

Selma was staring at the mud coloured object she held. She spoke in a voice that made her sister look up at her curiously.

"Laura, stop scrabbling. Come into the house."

There was something in the tone that made Laura obey. She scrambled out of the depression and followed her sister into the house. Selma closed the door behind them and then spoke.

"It *is* gold," she said. "Gold stays bright, no matter how long it's been buried. And I don't think these stones are semi-precious. They're real—and valuable."

"There! I said so! And there's more. Why can't we lift it out now? There's nobody there."

Laura's voice had dropped to a whisper.

"Why can't we go down and . . . "

141

"No." Selma spoke in her usual matter-of-fact manner. "No. The first thing we have to do is show these things to someone who knows more about them than we do."

"Who, for instance? Do you mean one of those experts who worked on the digging?"

"No. Someone who can tell us what they are, but who won't go round gossiping about them."

"Why shouldn't they gossip about them?"

"Simply because the fewer people who hear about this, the better. We shall say nothing except what is true: that we happened to pick them up."

"Don't we say that there's lots more to pick up?"

"No."

"But the diggers will find the rest, and . . . "

"Tomorrow is Saturday and they won't be working. Before they come back to work on Monday, we shall know more about our find."

"Who's going to tell us?"

Selma walked into the kitchen, pulled out a chair and sat down. Laura gazed at her expectantly from the doorway.

"Do you remember," Selma asked her, "the time, long ago, years ago, when Mrs. Lyle bought all those books about gold and jewels, and studied them to learn how to make copies?"

"Yes, I remember. She was going to make jewellery and sell it. But she found it too hard so she left off."

"The practical part was difficult, but she knew—she knows—enough to tell us whether these stones we've found are real, or just rubbish. We shall take them to her and see what she says."

Laura was frowning in concentration.

"Not the gold?"

"No. We know it is gold. It's the stones we don't know anything about. We merely . . . " Selma stood up. "Not we—leave me to do the talking. I'd rather you didn't say anything."

"All right. But when do we ask her?"

"Tomorrow. Not in the morning—Ward is always there in the morning. We'll wait until he and Philippa have gone away."

It was after tea that they made their way to Mrs. Lyle's house. In Selma's handbag, carefully wrapped in newspaper, with most, but not all of the mud removed, were the coloured stones they had unearthed.

It was at first disconcerting to find that Philippa was at home. But Selma, having rehearsed her part, was only momentarily put out. She and Laura were made welcome, and offered a second tea, refused, and settled down to what they called a nice little chat. This ranged over local affairs, with Selma making no reference whatsoever to the matter which had brought them. Laura watched her sister with what Philippa thought a strange intentness, but did not contribute to the conversation. Only when the sisters rose did Laura, in a nervous tone, venture a reminder.

"But Selma, didn't you want to ask . . . "

Selma gave her a quelling glance and complimented Philippa on the improvements that she and Ward were making in the town. Then, on her way to the door, she paused and turned to Mrs. Lyle.

"I almost forgot," she said. She opened her handbag and took out the small packages. "Laura and I happened to pick up these odds and ends of stones near the pavement excavation, and we wondered if you could tell us what they were."

Philippa took the package, walked to a small table, and opened them.

"Rather muddy, I'm afraid," Selma apologised. "But you can see them fairly clearly."

Mrs. Lyle had come to the table and was picking up

the coloured objects one by one. Selma and Laura watched her in silence.

"Beads?" Selma enquired at last.

Mrs. Lyle frowned.

"No. At least I don't think so. It'd hard to tell. They could be jewels. I've got some books upstairs I could bring down and . . . "

"Oh, no, don't trouble, please don't trouble," Selma broke in. "I merely asked because you knew something about jewellery."

"It's a fascinating subject." Mrs. Lyle's interest had quickened. "The jewels of the ancient Egyptians were very colourful—polychromatic—but in Greece the jewellers worked mostly in gold. Gold was used to mount precious stones because it didn't corrode. But peasant jewellery—in China for example—was mounted in silver."

Philippa was not listening. She was staring at the stones that had been laid neatly on the table, and something—a memory, a tantalising scrap of something heard or seen, began to form in her mind. Heard? No. Seen? Yes. But where? In a museum? No. Then . . .

Suddenly, with a feeling of unreality, she found herself transported in imagination to the gallery of the Manor. A portrait—a portrait of a woman. And round the woman's waist, a belt of gold chain encrusted with beautiful precious stones . . . There was no gold here, but surely those beautiful colours, the lovely shapes of the stones, were identical with those she had seen in the portrait?

With an effort, she brought herself back to the drawing room. Selma was rewrapping the stones, and Mrs. Lyle was speaking.

" . . . so I'd say they have no value, but you could show them to someone who's an expert in these things."

"Oh, I don't think it would be worth doing that," Selma replied. "One doesn't want to waste their time. I'm grateful to you for explaining that they're not really worth anything."

Mrs. Lyle saw the sisters to the door.

"Selma's very sensible," she said, on returning. "I don't think she'll bother to take those stones to any of the experts on the site. Ever since the excavating began, people have been finding rubbishy bits of stones or pottery and imagining they've unearthed a Roman treasure."

"Are you sure those stones had no value?" Philippa asked her. "They were beautiful."

"Yes, they were," her mother said. "But when I was studying the subject, I didn't go deeply enough into it to be able to make a judgment."

"But you did make a judgment," Philippa said. "You said they were worthless."

"That wasn't a judgment, it was merely an opinion," her mother objected. "That's all they asked me for, and that's all I could give them."

Philippa said no more; she felt it was useless to continue the discussion. What she wanted was to look at the portrait once more.

On their way back to the house, the sisters did not speak. Only when they were indoors did Selma address Laura.

"I believe," she said, "that the stones *are* valuable."

"Even though Mrs. Lyle said they weren't?"

"Yes. When she offered to look up the books she had on the subject, it suddenly struck me that it would be awkward, very awkward indeed, if the stones proved to be valuable. We were ill advised to take the stones to her, but there's no harm done. She's convinced that they're worthless."

145

"Then going there was a waste of time?"

"No. What she said about precious stones being mounted in gold made me feel sure that the little pieces of gold we found are part of a whole."

"Then can't we go down now and dig out the rest?" Laura enquired.

"No."

"Why not?"

"Because, unless we wait till it's dark, people will see us. And if we really did find anything of value, we would have to give it up."

"Well, we found the things, didn't we? Why should we give them up?"

Selma spoke in a tone of exasperation.

"I wish you'd *think* sometimes, Laura. Why did you think that I was so interested in these finds if I hadn't had a good reason for trying to find out something about them? Did you think I was doing all this for ourselves?"

"I knew you had something in mind, but I couldn't guess what it was."

"Then I'll tell you. Listen carefully."

Laura listened carefully.

"If by some extraordinary chance we find more of this gold," continued Selma, "then who would it belong to? Whose land has this been since goodness knows how long? Don't look bewildered, Laura. *Think*."

"The Rowallens."

"Exactly. So suppose—I'm only saying supposing —we found anything that Ward might turn into money do you want someone to come along and ask him to give it up?"

"No. You mean we ought to . . . to give it to him?"

"Who else? It's Ward's by right, and if there's anything valuable there, which is still problematical,

146

then Ward shall have it. As soon as it's dark, we shall put on our boots and wrap up warmly, and take a torch and a trowel and a bucket, and go and see what's there.''

They went out at midnight. Selma carried the torch and trowel, Laura held the bucket. Cautiously, they dug into the side of the trench, first at a low level and then, finding nothing, began to probe halfway up the slope.

After the first gasp from Laura, when they came upon the first gleam, they made no sound. They shook away soil, and gently deposited their finds in the bucket. Not until they had assured themselves that no more was to be found did they stop, and get to their feet, and ease their cramped limbs.

''That's all,'' whispered Selma. ''Now come indoors.''

Laura paused to grovel once more.

''There's no more, Laura.''

''No. I just thought . . . do you know, Selma, there's a bone down there.''

''We are not collecting bones. Will you please come away. Shine the torch here, but keep it low.''

Laura followed her. They carried the bucket to the kitchen, spread newspapers on the floor and carefully lifted out the objects from the soil. They laid line after line of beautifully coloured stones on the paper. They put together the separate pieces of gold mesh. Then they drew up two chairs and sat gazing at their handiwork.

''I don't care what you or Mrs. Lyle or anybody else says,'' Laura said definitely at last. ''I say these are jewels. Not semi-precious stones. *Precious* stones.''

''If they are, then we *have* found a treasure. And it's Ward's. We shall ask him to come in tomorrow and look at what we've found, and he'll know whether it's valuable or not. And now come to bed.''

147

"Leaving it all on the newspaper?"

"Yes."

"Without cleaning it up or anything?"

"He can see it just as it is. Would you like a hot drink to make you sleep?"

"No. Would you?"

Neither wanted anything. They removed their boots and their coats and went upstairs to bed. Both, tired after their exertions, fell asleep almost immediately. But some hours later, Selma was roused by a sound, and by the faint light of dawn discerned in the doorway of her bedroom a large form.

"Laura, what on earth . . ."

She switched on the light. Laura came in and stood by her bed, a look of distress on her face.

"What is it, Laura?"

"I was asleep, and I woke up and I began to think about . . . about what we'd found, and then I remembered . . ."

"Remembered what?"

"It *isn't* Ward's and they *could* make us give it up."

Her gaze, under the net nightcap, rested on Selma expectantly. She did not have long to wait. Selma sat up in bed and spoke.

"You're right, of course. He sold that land—this land. It isn't his any more. So . . ."

"So that means, doesn't it, that whatever's underneath it belongs to whoever bought it? That means the town. Do we have to give up things to them that really belong to Ward?"

There was scarcely a pause.

"No. We don't," said Selma firmly.

"But I don't see . . ."

"Sit down. We've got to think this over."

Laura sat on the side of the bed. For some time, there

was silence. The brows of both sisters were knitted in deep thought.

"We could ask Ward to . . . " began Laura.

"No. Ward mustn't come into this," interrupted Selma.

"But you've just said, we've just said those things, whatever they are, belong to him, so . . . "

"If he knew where we found them, he'd know they didn't belong to him. So we mustn't tell him."

"But . . . "

"He's got to find them himself."

"What difference does that make, Selma? The only way he can say they're his is if they were on, I mean under, his own land, and the only land he's got is the Manor grounds."

"Exactly. So that's where he must find them," said Selma.

Laura took in the words and began the slow, arduous process of trying to understand them.

"You'll have to explain," she said at last.

"What is there to explain? We've just said that Ward must find those things on his own grounds."

"Yes, I know. But—but they're not there."

"We shall put them there."

Laura could only stare. Selma spoke impatiently.

"Go back to bed. You'll catch your death."

"Put them there? But . . . how?"

"I shall think of something," Selma said.

"There's a full moon on Thursday. We could . . . "

"We don't want a full moon, we want clouds."

There was a long silence.

"We could go in the daytime," Laura said at last.

"Don't be *silly,* Laura. How could we walk over to the Manor, carrying those things in full view?"

"I didn't mean in full view. I meant the way we take buckets to Mrs. Lyle, to ask her for cuttings. Nobody would know we weren't carrying cuttings, would they?"

Selma, speechless, stared at her. Laura was not given to making sensible suggestions. As for coming out with a real idea, an idea that seemed more and more brilliant as Selma examined it, this was something that had not happened since their youth.

The lack of response reduced Laura to her wonted humility.

"I don't suppose it was worth mentioning," she said, abashed. "I just thought . . . "

"It's a magnificent idea, and I'm ashamed of myself for not thinking of it," said Selma warmly. "It's the obvious solution. We need cuttings, we ask permission to take cuttings, we go up to the Manor and we take our buckets and trowels and some cuttings of our own."

"So that there'll be mud in the buckets to hide the . . . "

"Yes."

"But where, exactly, are we going to put them?"

"I'll think of something. As close as possible to the edge of the property."

"But how will people know where they are? I mean . . . "

"I know exactly what you mean. You feel that there should be a pointer, a clue, shall we call it?"

"Yes. Otherwise, they might be buried for years—centuries."

"We must make sure that they're not."

"We could leave some of them showing."

"Certainly not. They might fall into the wrong hands. They must be found by Ward, and Ward only."

"That's going to be difficult," Laura said despondently.

But it proved not at all difficult. When the sisters, in their little car, set out for school next morning, they passed a group of workmen with ladders and axes making their way to the Manor. Selma stopped the car and addressed the leader.

"More tree topping, Mr. Todd?" she enquired.

"S'right," Mr. Todd replied through the twig he was chewing. "Up at the big house."

"And how many this time?"

"Four, five, likely as not. We'll start with the big oak that's blocking the view from the dining room west window. After that, we'll tackle the smaller chaps on the edge of the drive."

Selma nodded and drove on.

"Providential," she remarked to her sister.

"I don't see . . ."

"Never mind now. I'll explain when we get home this evening."

"You mean we can choose any of the trees that have been lopped, because Ward is bound to go out and look at them?"

Selma felt a surge of sisterly pride. In Laura, such percipience amounted almost to divination.

"That's right, dear," she said.

Philippa also met the workmen; like them, she was on her way to the Manor. Ward was on his way down. When they met, she told him that she had come to look —with his permission—at one of the pictures in the gallery.

He turned and walked with her up the hill.

"Any particular picture?" he asked.

"Yes."

"Which?"

"The picture of the runaway bride—the wife of the ninth baronet."

They went inside, and in the gallery she stood looking at the jewel-encrusted belt. The colour and the shape of the stones seemed to her to be very much like the ones that the Plessey sisters had found—but it was impossible to judge, impossible to be certain.

"What's interesting you about the runaway bride?" Ward enquired at last.

She sat on one of the benches opposite the picture.

"The Plesseys found some coloured stones and brought them to my mother to see if they had any value. My mother thought they hadn't, and said so—but, as you no doubt know, her researches into the hobbies she takes up and then drops are pretty shallow. If the Plesseys expected to learn anything from her they went away disappointed."

"What made you form an opinion different to your mother's?"

"I don't know. It sounds silly, but I had a feeling I'd seen something like them before. As I was staring at them, I remembered the belt, and I wanted to come and look at it again."

"Where did the Plesseys find the stones?"

"Near where they're digging to uncover the pavement."

"How many were there?"

"I didn't count. About eight, I think. But they were beautiful, and they were all shaped differently, and I couldn't believe they were worthless. I think they ought to be shown to someone who knows something about them."

He sat down at her side.

"You weren't here when they were doing the main excavations," he said. "If you had been, you would have known that every week, almost every day, someone picked up a fragment of this or that and made a beeline for the nearest expert to ask its value. The experts were harassed, the museum was besieged and . . ."

"The whole thing began because you found a fragment."

"True. But before going to the experts I spent a lot of time in the British Museum and I consulted important works on the subject. Once the excavating began, a close watch was kept on the work and the workers."

"They haven't been digging under the Plesseys' garden for long. How do you know that they mightn't have picked up something that the experts missed?"

"If they did, they should have the stones examined—after which they'll be the property of the town. If you're keen on helping them to find out more about the stones, I'll speak to one of the . . . "

"No. Since seeing the things, I hadn't really thought of the Plesseys—I wanted to prove to myself that I'd let my imagination run away with me." She turned and faced him. "You've never been really interested in the story, have you?"

"The story of the runaway wife? No. There didn't seem anything to underpin the bald facts. She ran away. Her husband saw her and her gentleman friend, and set out to catch them, but on the way over the rotting bridge fell in and he was drowned. When I was young I used to come into this gallery on wet days and sometimes I wondered if it would be possible to find out anything about who and what she was before her marriage, but her origins were obscure and the only interesting fact about her seemed to be the number of continental princes—princelings—who fell under her spell."

"Didn't anybody ever find out where the two of them went?"

"No. Investigations moved slowly in those days. They obviously left the country, which meant making for one of the nearest ports. But nobody ever saw them, and no owner of any barque or packet or anything else admitted having taken them on as passengers. That's about as far as the search went. None of my relations seemed unduly interested in the incident—I mean the relations I've known."

"But a belt worth a fortune . . . "

"We're not by any means the only family—old or new—to have lost a fortune. You can have all your valuable assets, portable ones, carried off by thieves. You can lose a fortune by bad speculation. You can be swindled out of a fortune by confidence tricksters. We were unlucky because the belt was at the same time priceless and portable. But to return to your problem— I don't think that there's the slightest possibility that any of the stones in it could by any chance have been found here. The lovers fled far and fast. Do you want me to look at the stones the Plesseys found?"

She hesitated.

"No. I think they regretted asking my mother about them. They'll probably clean them up and show them to one of their relations—Lord Basquine, maybe." She looked up at the portrait. "I suppose if the ninth baronet gave it to her . . . "

"It wasn't the ninth baronet's to give. Not give as he did, outright. Family jewels are family jewels and should go down to the up-and-coming generations."

"A kind of trust, yes. I've always been glad my family didn't have a crock of gold. When you've nothing much to lose, nothing much to tempt the robber bands, you can relax. Look at poor Mr. Mac-Robert, with his nose for ever in the *Financial Times,* finding out what's happened to his investments."

"Poor is hardly the word I'd apply to our friend MacRobert. If you've finished looking at portraits, why don't we take a look at the lovely sunshine outside?"

She rose and they walked down the hill together. She paused to look back at the lovely old house.

"Yes, it's a nice place." Ward was following her unspoken thought. "Just think what we could do in the way of restoration if only we had a nice gold belt."

8

"Had a nice day?" Philippa asked her mother when she went into her room to say good night the following night.

"Very nice. It's been quiet—the Plesseys were here taking cuttings for their garden. And you?"

"I've been busy."

"Doing what?"

"Arranging to open a new café. Getting the two owners together."

"Why two owners?"

"Mr. Laforge, who as you know runs the restaurant nearest to the Ridge, is worried about competition."

"Why? He's doing pretty well, isn't he?"

"He's doing very well—largely because he had a sort of monopoly of all the tourists who came to see the villa. With a café opening practically on the site, he felt . . . "

"How could a café open any nearer to the site than his restaurant? There's no building available for a nearer one."

Philippa smiled, and her mother realised she was keeping something back.

"You're hiding something," she said.

155

"Yes, but you could guess if you tried. What building is there between the site and Laforge's restaurant?"

"There's the Beethams'—the MacRoberts'—house, and the Armitages . . ."

"Right. The MacRoberts aren't likely to open a restaurant. So that leaves . . . ?"

"The Armitages. Don't tell me they're giving up their house?"

"Why should they give up their house?"

Mrs. Lyle frowned.

"Look, if you've got some news, I'd like to hear it."

"You can't guess?"

"No."

"Then I'll tell you. How often have you heard Mr. Armitage moan and groan because he felt he was too young to retire? Don't bother to answer that. He isn't going to retire. He's going to keep on working. But not at accountancy. Justin is going on with the accountancy. His father William is going to turn the lower floor of his house into an establishment to be known as the Sandwich Bar—he wouldn't consider any more fancy names, even from Mr. Laforge, who's going to be his partner for three years."

There was a pause.

"I don't believe it," Mrs. Lyle said flatly. "It's just a rumour. If it had been in his mind—which I can't believe—he would have told me."

"He wanted to tell you. More than once, when the negotiations were going on, he told me that he hated the thought that he hadn't been able to tell you what he was going to do. But it had to be kept secret."

"Would I have shouted it from the housetops?"

"No, you wouldn't. But people had begun to guess what was being planned, and . . ."

"I'm very angry with him," said Mrs. Lyle.

"Don't be angry, just wish him luck."

"But how can an accountant make a success of a sandwich bar?"

"Anybody can make a success of a sandwich bar—if they start as William is doing, with a flock of practically on-the-spot customers, and if they have the flair for providing tasty food that William has."

"Only sandwiches?"

"Mainly sandwiches. And cool drinks—Justin's speciality—in summer, and cold beer especially for the bus and coach drivers when they bring in the customers and hot soups in those huge cups that William's been collecting for years, and of course ice cream. Mr. Laforge is going to do the ices."

"Those downstairs rooms of William's can't accommodate . . . "

"Yes, they can, or they will. They're being made into one enormous hall, with a counter and stools all round. William's two garages are being turned into loos."

"Great heavens! What a mercy the Beethams had already decided to leave. Will Mr. MacRobert object?"

"No. They're out of sight, discreetly sheltered by greenery. So will you be nice to William, and tell him how pleased you are?"

"Yes. Does he need any extra barmaids?"

"Ask him."

Her mother gave a loud sigh.

"Oh, Philippa, Philippa, what has happened to the Ridge? So many years of peace, of neighbourliness, and now . . . "

"And now changes, and in a way I'm glad." Philippa rose from her place at the edge of the bed, and bent to kiss her mother. "You'll have so much more to be part of when I've gone away."

The Ridge was indeed in turmoil. The years of inactivity were over, and at every house preparations could be

157

seen being made for a new way of life. The Beethams were giving a series of farewell parties that included most of the notables of the town. Mr. MacRobert had imported an architect from London and plans were being made for an expensive conversion.

Mr. and Mrs. Luton were seldom seen; they were engaged in packing up everything that belonged to them and, as it transpired later, a great deal that did not. Denise was busy packing up the contents of Reid's flat; in the intervals of helping her, Reid looked forward to restoring the little swimming pool of the Ridge house—which Mrs. Luton had filled with ornamental fish—to its original function. He was determined to clean and scrape and paint and fill and filter until the water shone pale green and inviting.

The Plesseys, in between gathering cuttings and storing them in Mrs. Lyle's garden, were occupied in arranging the final stages of their end-of-term play. This, a dramatic conflict between early Christians and Roman pagans, they had hoped to stage on the site of the Roman villa. Permission had been obtained, but the preliminary rehearsals had made it clear that letting forty or more young children loose among the excavations called for a peace-keeping force larger than the Plesseys could assemble. But the idea had raised the town's interest in the play and so many tickets had been sold that it had been decided to engage the Pilgrims' Hall, which had the largest stage and auditorium in the district. The teams of scene-shifting fathers and other backstage assistants had been greatly augmented and Ward confided to Philippa that there were going to be more assistants than actors and actresses.

Philippa was packing, and also going through the house in the vain hope of persuading her mother to throw out useless but cherished articles. The Springers were basking in the glory of having a son who had kicked the two goals that had placed his team first in the queue for Wembley.

Philippa's days were full—too full to allow her leisure to count the days that remained before her departure. She had little time left. The few weeks since her return had flown with a speed that left her under no illusions as to the correspondingly swift approach of her departure. But there was work to fill every hour of the day. There were visits in the town with Ward, meetings with a variety of professional men and women who were following Ward's lead in attempts to improve the amenities of Montoak. There were expeditions to meet out-of-town tradespeople—these Philippa found the most interesting of all their contacts. She and Ward, anxious to make the most of the sunshine, had brought their long-stored bicycles into use, and after much scraping and tyre mending and frame polishing, had taken to pedalling round the countryside. They took packed lunches which they ate outside rural inns; they stopped at out-of-the-way pubs for beer or cider and got home in time for dinner, hungry, tired and frequently rainwashed.

Philippa wrote accounts of these outings for Dudley each night. Putting the letters into the envelopes, she tried in vain to understand exactly how Ward had contrived to keep their relationship on a cool and friendly basis and at the same time leave her in no doubt that this was his way of keeping her aware of himself and his feelings. Except for their picnic lunches, they were seldom alone—but, though their association could be called intimate, this was not something she allowed her mind to dwell on. He was Ward, the perfect companion, the fast-becoming-indispensable escort. She could, she knew, bring the meetings to an end. She could decide that she was endangering her relationship with Dudley, and she could refuse to continue the work

159

she was helping Ward to do. But the days went by and found her still packing lunches, still setting out by car or bicycle or on foot for another day with Ward.

They ran into Justin one day as they were walking to the car park. He stopped, and put a question.

"Heard the news about the *Montoak Mail*?" he asked them.

"Sold?" Ward asked.

"Yes. You knew?"

"I knew MacRobert was proposing to buy it. What's he going to do—appoint a new staff?"

"I'm in a hurry, or I'd stop and tell you a few details. Get hold of Guy—he's just been seeing MacRobert."

They had to look a long time for Guy. The landlord of every pub at which they enquired had the same answer: "He was here a short time ago—he's just left."

They located him when they had given up the search and were driving back to the Ridge. He was seated in his car under the entrance archway, motionless, gazing at the scenery. They had to address him several times before he recognised them.

"Well, well, well. So it's you," he told them at last. "I was just going to pay the Manor a visit. I was waiting for some of the beer fumes to disperse. Do I smell like a saloon bar?"

"Yes. We'll overlook it," Ward said, "if you'll follow me home and tell me what's happened."

In the garden of the Manor, sharing the shaky, ill balanced bench under an oak tree, he told them.

"Sold. For a song, as I said it would be. I haven't seen old Walters, but I saw his wife, who said that thirty years had been lifted from her husband's shoulders, whatever that means."

"And the staff?" Philippa enquired.

"Not a sweeping out," Guy answered, "just a weeding out. And though I don't like MacRobert, I'll admit that he's got good judgment. He knew which the weeds were, and he's pulling them out and leaving the sturdier plants. Maybe he's been round making a few enquiries, but whatever it was, he's keeping the cream. And that includes me. He called me into his office—Walters' office—and in twelve minutes flat he told me what he thought of me, not flattering, of my attainments, somewhat more complimentary, and of my work, of which he spoke highly. He went on to tell me that he'd leave me alone if I followed his general line. He raised my salary, and that made me a bit lightheaded, so I didn't hear what he said next. He had to repeat it. I'm the new Editor, he told me, and then he told me to get out and get to work.''

"What were you doing in all those pubs—working?" Philippa asked.

"Celebrating. Thanking God, from whom all editorial blessings flow. I'm the Editor-in-Chief of the *Montoak Mail*." He stood up, causing Ward and Philippa to slide to the ground. "I'm the *Montoak Mail*'s Editor-in-Chief, and I'm going to get out of that garret I'm in and find myself an abode worthy of my new status."

Ward was helping Philippa to her feet.

"You can ask the Plesseys to take you in," he suggested. "They'll have a spare room and bath, and they can do with the money."

"That's a good idea," Guy said. "I'll go now."

"I'd wait a bit if I were you," Ward told him. "They're appointing assistants for their play. Justin's been caught to do the lighting. I'm prompter. Philippa and her mother are wardrobe mistresses."

"They can't rope me in." Guy was leaving. "Not an Editor-in-Chief. It was different when I was a mere reporter, sitting in the background doing a write-up. So long. Ring for an appointment if you want to see me."

9

Philippa was still packing. But it was packing of an unusual nature. Having carefully folded some clothes and placed them in the suitcase, she took them out again and replaced them in drawers. This process, at brief intervals, was repeated so often that at last Mrs. Lyle, who, when embarking on a new hobby, was not disposed to notice anything that took place outside her workroom, was driven to enquire the reason for this odd behaviour.

Before enquiring, however, she studied her daughter and saw much that had escaped her notice in the past weeks. She went to Philippa's bedroom early one morning, and found her dressed and seated at her writing table. Before her was a blank sheet of paper, at her feet was a wastepaper basket overflowing with letters begun and torn up.

Mrs. Lyle sat on the bed and gazed at the discarded efforts. There was silence in the room. Philippa seemed to be in a daydream; she had not turned her head at her mother's entrance.

Mrs. Lyle spoke at last.

"Philippa, if there's anything wrong, can't you tell me about it? I might be able to help."

Philippa faced her.

"Nobody can help," she said. "I got myself into this, and I've got to get myself out."

"Out of what?" Mrs. Lyle grew pale. "Out of your . . . engagement?"

"Yes."

"You're . . . you're writing to Dudley?"

"Yes."

"To . . . to tell him . . . "

"To tell him what I should have told him weeks ago —that I can't marry him."

Silence fell once more.

"Is it . . . Ward?" Mrs. Lyle asked at last.

Philippa rose, walked to the open window, and stood staring out.

"I don't know," she said. "Yes, I do know, but I don't seem to be able to think straight any more. What I'd like more than anything is to find some woman who's been in a similar situation and ask her what she did about it."

"Are you saying that you love Ward and not Dudley?"

"I wish it was as easy as that." Philippa turned and leaned on the window sill. "I wish it was a straightforward situation like that. But it isn't."

"Darling . . . " Her mother spoke gently. "It's hard to tell a man you've changed your mind, but in a case like this it has to be done."

"I've just said that it should have been done weeks ago."

"Why have you waited till now?"

"Because I couldn't believe it had happened. I hadn't the courage to face a picture of myself as a woman who could promise a man to marry him and then almost immediately meet another man and realise—or imagine—she was in love with him. I'm not sure of anything any more—not sure of myself."

Mrs. Lyle was frowning.

"But before you went to Canada . . . "

"There was nothing. And no warning that when I saw him again, I'd feel as I did . . . as I do."

"Does he know how you feel?"

"He does by now."

"But if he knows, then . . . "

" . . . then he's waiting for me to tell him, and to tell Dudley." She stared unseeingly across the room. "So easy—on paper. Make your decision, choose the man you want, and that's all. But when the two men are Ward and Dudley, when I've been the fool I was in giving Dudley a promise before I left Canada . . . "

"Nobody said it was easy, Philippa darling, but it has to be done."

"Yes. And in doing it, I hurt bitterly, perhaps for all his life, a man who's kind, decent, reliable, who's over there getting our home ready, who waited patiently for me to make up my mind to marry him, who's a man any woman in her senses would be proud to marry. What's Ward? Decent, yes. Patient, yes. Reliable? He . . . "

"Most certainly reliable." Mrs. Lyle broke in in a firm voice. "Most certainly a man you can trust and lean on. A man . . . "

"A man who's never held down a regular job, who's content to go on living on a mere trickle of money, who has no plans for the future, who has got along because he's got that damned, overvalued quality called charm. The woman who marries him is going to be conducted to a leaking, almost unfurnished house, and asked to make the best of it."

"If you're going to choose by material standards . . . "

"How can I choose? At this moment, I feel that I've chosen. I love Ward. What I felt for Dudley was affection. What I feel for Ward is . . . how can I explain? I'm not 'in love'. My feeling for Ward is so deep, so sure, that I know with certainty that whatever happens to us in the future, I'll love him as I do now. He's part of my whole life. My memories of him go back to the time I was allowed to join the Ridge gang

164

and he was part of it whenever he was in England. Being with him is like being at home, familiar, safe. But what I can't forget is that when I left Canada, I was quite happy to go back and live there and marry Dudley. I didn't ever feel about him as I feel about Ward—but I felt enough to be sure I'd be happy with him. So when you say choose . . . ''

"You can't let him come here, Philippa, without . . . ''

"I can't let him come here until I've had more time to get my mind straightened out. I can't face him feeling as I do now—torn in two. I want to write and ask for a little more time.''

"But if you do that, he'll realise . . . ''

"Yes. Perhaps he will. But he's too decent a man, and I'm too fond of him, to let him come over believing that things are as they were when I left him. I couldn't. I wouldn't have the courage to face him with the truth. Just imagine—coming here to fetch a bride and finding that she . . . '' She stopped and met the troubled, tearful eyes of her mother. "There's nothing for you to worry about,'' she said gently.

She went over to her and put her arms round her.

"Talking to you has helped,'' she said. "I'll write to Dudley tonight and tell him the truth.''

"Which is?''

"That I think I'm in love, I'm *sure* I'm in love with Ward.''

"That's not asking for more time to think things over.''

"It's giving him a chance to change his mind—if he wants to. It's bringing him into the picture. He's patient, and he's understanding, so maybe he'll convince me that what I feel for Ward is the natural result of coming home and . . . '' Once more she stopped. "What, what, what can I say to him?''

"Whatever you say, Philippa, say it at once. Write the letter now."

"I'll write it tonight."

"Why wait till tonight? Write now, at once."

"No. Tonight. My mind'll be clearer then."

"You've forgotten," said Mrs. Lyle, "that there's a party tonight."

"Yes, I'd forgotten," Philippa admitted. "When it's over, I'll write the letter."

On the day that Reid and Denise fixed their wedding day, Mrs. Lyle had suggested giving them a party. In spite of the short notice, all their friends attended. Guests brought generous contributions to the feast. Old friends met new friends—van drivers mingled with maîtres d'hôtel and café owners; the Chesters came to serve the drinks and ended up as guests. The drawing room, the adjacent kitchen, the hall and the dining room were filled with a company who were dislodged only when the supply of food and drink ran out.

When only Mrs. Lyle, Ward and Philippa were left with the two guests of honour, Reid spoke feelingly.

"I don't think I ever enjoyed myself so much," he declared. "Thanks, Phil. Thanks, Mrs. Lyle. I thought mixing people up in the way you did tonight might not . . . well, come off. But it did. Now let's start clearing up."

The clearing up, with so many willing hands, did not take long. Glasses and plates were washed and put away, the rooms were tidied and furniture put in place.

"If anybody has any space to fit dinner," said Reid, "I'm willing to provide it. Why don't we . . . "

He stopped. The telephone was ringing in the hall.

"Hope it's not a job for me," he said apprehensively. "I'm not in any state to drive a van."

Philippa had gone out to answer, leaving the door

166

open. The conversation in the room began again, only to be checked by Philippa's incredulous voice.

"*Dudley*? *Where*? You mean you're in London . . .? How . . . ?"

There was an interval as he explained. Then she spoke briefly.

"There's a train getting to Ashford from here in just over an hour. I'll meet you there."

She put down the receiver and re-entered the room. She seemed to have difficulty in focusing on the group watching her.

"Dudley," she said. "I'm meeting him at Ashford." Her eyes went to her mother. "I'll go up and finish getting his room ready."

Her mother had risen.

"No, you won't. You'll go for that train," she said. "I'll do the room."

"Can I help?" asked Denise.

"No, thank you."

Philippa went as far as the door and turned.

"I'm sorry to break this up," she said, and seemed about to say more, but changed her mind. She and her mother went upstairs and Philippa's door closed.

In the drawing room, Reid looked at Ward.

"Can I take you anywhere in town?" he asked.

Ward shook his head.

"No, thanks. If anybody wants me—which they won't—they'll find me in my house on the hill. See you sometime."

He went out, and they heard his footsteps going down the steps and into the road. Denise looked at Reid.

"What did I tell you?" she said.

"I don't remember what you told me. Did you guess he'd be turning up ahead of time?"

"I didn't guess, but if he was a man who knew

167

anything at all about women, he should have shown up some time ago."

"If you ask me . . . " Reid began.

Denise spoke with unaccustomed tartness.

"I didn't ask you," she said. "Come on, let's get going."

"I came," Dudley was saying as he drove Philippa homeward, "to find out where you'd gone to. I tried to come earlier, but I couldn't get away."

He spoke in his habitual, calm matter-of-fact manner. They were driving from Ashford to Montoak. Every now and then he turned his gaze from the road ahead to study her expression. She had said little since their meeting at Ashford; she had kissed him with a warmth that had reassured him, because he did not know how much relief she had felt when his arms were round her. He was here. There would be no more problems. He represented the signpost at the crossroads—the signpost that pointed West, the finger that indicated the future. The interval at home was over, and she could no longer call this place home. Home would be where Dudley was.

He stopped the car and took one of her hands lightly in his own.

"Did you know you'd gone away?" he asked.

"I know my letters were . . . hollow."

"Hollow isn't a bad description."

"I found it impossible . . . to paint any sort of picture."

"I sensed that. What I couldn't figure out was what had got in the way. Something had sent me rolling into the distance like a ball in one of those croquet games my grandmother used to win prizes at. Then I got to thinking that maybe it wasn't myself that was receding into the distance. Maybe it was you. So I came to find out."

Too moved to speak, she drew his hand up to rest for a moment on her cheek.

"I was right to come," he said out of a long silence. "Wasn't I? I was right to come now."

"If you mean that by coming now you would have more time to get a clearer picture of things here, then, yes, you were right."

He drew a finger gently across her cheek.

"What blurred the picture for you?" he asked.

She answered unhesitatingly.

"Being here. Just being here. I didn't expect to fall straight back into my old life. I came to see my mother and to . . . ."

" . . . to sever old ties?"

"Yes. I thought of myself as a kind of visitor, but that wasn't how it turned out. Being back meant being part of it all again."

"These are your roots," he told her gently. "You put down deep roots."

Deeper, he thought, than he had realised. He took her hand—it lay inert in his. He took her in his arms—she returned his kiss, but he knew that there was no passion in it.

He had always known—feared—that there were passionate depths in her which he had failed to reach. Now he had to face the fact that this other man, who had figured so largely in her letters, this Rowallen with whom she had spent so much of her time, might have succeeded where he himself had failed.

"Roots can be pulled up," he heard her saying.

"Yes, they can." He hesitated. "But I don't want you to feel bound to marry me unless you're absolutely sure you want to. When you left Canada, you were sure. At least, I was sure. But every one of your letters made me less sure. They were written, or it seemed to me that they were written, from a sense of duty. That

169

frightened me. So I came over, but I haven't come to claim anything you don't want to give me. All I want is to find the girl I loved and thought I knew well. That's all."

Tears were running down her cheeks. He wiped them away.

"There's nothing to worry about," he said gently. "For the moment, I'm happy just to be near you. Everything else can wait."

Can wait . . . can wait . . . can wait . . . The words echoed in her ears, in her mind. Everything else . . .

And Ward, she knew, was waiting.

After a long silence, she heard Dudley speaking.

"I'm going to make a suggestion," he said. "You can take your time thinking it over—but I think it makes sense."

"What is it?"

He spoke calmly, and without any sign of the effort he was making in putting his proposal to her.

"It's this. Instead of our getting married as soon as we get to Canada, I think you ought to stay with your father for a short spell—to do some thinking. We shall see one another as often as we want to, but the thing that both of us have got to find out is exactly where you belong. Coming back here, your first letters showed plainly that your time in Canada had been, in a sense, an . . . an episode. You hadn't, as I'd thought, as I'd hoped, as I'd believed, integrated. You had remained outside."

"Dudley, I . . . "

"Wait a minute. There isn't much more. You've got to give yourself time—I've got to give you time—to find out which side of the Atlantic you want to be on for the rest of your life. We've got to know, you and I both, whether the fact of loving me is going to compensate for all the things you love and have grown up with here.

170

When you promised to marry me, you had had two years in which to get a feeling of belonging—I can't put it any better than that. You had almost got England out of your system. Or so I believed. But when you hesitated about giving me an answer when I first asked you to marry me, I should have recognised the warning signs. I didn't. But I've seen them since, and that's why I'm here. I love you and I think you love me, but the way you feel for me mightn't be enough to give you absolute surety, absolute confidence in marrying me. So will you agree to leave things just as they are, and come back to Canada with me, saying nothing about our future to anybody here, and just making the final decision when you've had time to get the feel of the country again. Does that sound like good sense?''

It sounded to her like the most generous offer any man in love had ever brought himself to make. She tried to thank him, but she was incapable of speech. She lay in his arms, gratitude and relief almost overwhelming her. When he released her, he set the car in motion and they went in the direction of home.

It was going to be difficult—it was going to be almost impossible, she knew, to say nothing to Ward of the suggestion that Dudley had made. But neither to Ward nor to her mother, she resolved, would she speak of the plan. So much, at least, she owed Dudley.

10

Making Dudley's breakfast on the morning after his arrival, Philippa decided that in this scene Ward could have no place. He would no longer appear for breakfast. He had once said that he was filling in for Dudley. There was no longer any gap to fill. The cast was complete: mother, daughter, future son-in-law. The scene was a room filled with morning sunshine; the table was laid for breakfast. The dialogue was not flowing as it had flowed on previous mornings, but her mother's tranquillity and Dudley's easy silences gave her a sense of peace. No, Ward would not fit into this scene. She tried desperately to imagine future mornings, future days and evenings, to imagine life without him. She longed to go up the hill and bring him down with his sheaf of papers and discuss over their breakfast the work they were to do that day. But this, she told herself, was a feeling which sprang from the habits they had formed together. Habits were easily broken—and today was a good day to begin.

And then there were footsteps in the hall, and Ward was at the door and with a nod to Mrs. Lyle and Philippa was advancing and preventing Dudley from rising.

"Don't get up. My name's Rowallen and I'm a kind of adjunct to this family. I also represent the Welcome Committee of the Ridge."

Dudley, on his feet, was shaking hands.

"Philippa told me about you," he said in his slow, quiet voice. "You're the boss of the spread"—he nodded towards the window—"out there."

"Self-appointed boss." Philippa, with an effort, subdued her surge of happiness. "Ward, if you want coffee, help yourself."

"Thanks." He got a cup and saucer from the kitchen, every movement indicating his familiarity with the house and its arrangements. "Can I make toast for anyone else? I'm hungry—I've been swimming."

"I think we're through," Dudley said.

Philippa could see, without looking, the complete contrast that the two men made. Dudley was in grey trousers and a blue and white shirt in small checks; his jacket hung on the back of his chair. Ward was in jeans and a dark blue, open necked shirt, his hair still damp from his swim. The skins of both men were freshly shaven, smooth and healthy.

The atmosphere was relaxed and friendly. She had been wrong not to expect Ward, Philippa decided. With him added to the scene now, she felt it to be even more complete. Mother, daughter, future son-in-law and old family friend.

Dudley had left the table and was standing by the window, looking down on the villa. Ward spoke from the table.

"I'd like to be the one to show you round," he told him. "The place is full of amateur guides. They even sell pamphlets—the whole thing has escalated and is now more commerce than art. Philippa claims to know a lot of Roman history, but I wouldn't take that too seriously if I were you."

Dudley spoke with his eyes still on the villa.

"She was right when she said that you had to see it before you could believe it."

"We have to keep telling ourselves—by we I mean this town," said Ward, "that this isn't a unique show-piece. You can see Roman villas—if you have time to go and look—at Lullingstone and Chedworth and Bignor

173

and places west. At Brading, there's even a collection of tiles and coins that rivals ours. But where we score is the layout—as you've just discovered. The whole thing, villa, baths, pavements—on foundations that were laid over a thousand years ago.'' He had finished his toast; he filled his coffee cup, left it on the table and began to carry the rest of the cups and plates into the kitchen, continuing as he went. ''We're getting used to being famous.''

Dudley waited for him to return.

''How many people come to see the site—daily, weekly?'' he asked.

''I can get you the figures. I make my own estimate from the number of cars and buses in the car park every day. Yesterday there were eighteen cars and eight buses. Given time and a computer Philippa could multiply the cars by four and the buses by thirty and come up with an approximate answer. By the way, would you agree, while you're here, to serve on a panel of gastronomic judges? Philippa says you're a good judge of food—and wine. She can guide you round the restaurants and you could keep the score; so many marks for bar service, table service, food, wine and so on.''

''We could make it a foursome,'' Dudley suggested, his eyes on Mrs. Lyle. ''I'm told you never go out, but maybe you'd make an exception for me. How else can we get to know each other before I have to go back?''

''The trouble is,'' she explained, ''that when I go out to eat, I don't eat. Ward's done a lot to improve the restaurant standards, but even the new food is wasted on me. It's silly to sit looking at an empty plate all the evening. But I might . . . ''

She paused. Denise had called from the hall. A moment later she was in the doorway, her eyes on Dudley, a wide smile of welcome on her lips. She went forward and seized his hands.

"Hello, Dudley. I'm Denise Luton, and if Philippa didn't tell you about me, she should have done. My fiancé'll be here in a minute. I couldn't wait for him—I wanted to see you." She freed his hands and made a token greeting to the other three. "When you get engaged to a girl," she went on to Dudley, "you have to stand up and be inspected by all her friends and relations, and it's nice of you to have come early to give us a chance to get to know you. Did you have a good flight?"

"Yes, thank you. You're just as I pictured."

"I didn't picture you. Nobody here could. All Philippa said was: Wait and you'll see him soon. Did she tell you that I'm marrying a cockney? You know about cockneys?"

"I've met a few. But isn't every Londoner a cockney if he's born within the sound of Bow bells?"

"So they claim. It's not considered smart to talk like one, but then the Springers aren't smart; they're just nice." She looked at Ward's damp hair. "Were you swimming this morning?"

"Yes."

"You mean there's still water coming into that pond?"

"Yes. Not exactly a cascade, but it's flowing." He turned to Dudley. "It's interesting—at least, I think you'll find it is. A stream that's been dry, dammed, diverted—nobody knows for certain which yet—is reappearing. I think it's going to give trouble when the diggers uncover more of that Roman pavement they've located. You'll be able to look when we go over the site. Denise, I suppose you realise that I've lost my assistant?"

"You mean that you can't get Philippa to do your work for you any more. If you're counting on me, don't."

175

"All I'm asking you to . . . "

"The answer's no. I start work in Reid's office as from next Monday."

Reid, coming in, confirmed this. His greeting to Dudley was uttered in three careless words, after which he merged into the casual friendly atmosphere like a tributary flowing into a river.

An unexpected element in the situation was the instant and genuine liking that sprang up between Ward and Dudley. Dudley, deeply interested in the Roman villa, sought information on its discovery and excavation, and nobody was in a better position to supply it than Ward. The two, with Philippa, spent all their days together, forming a trio that, after a few days of mild surprise, everybody took for granted. They were sometimes on the site, sometimes interviewing shopkeepers and restauranteurs in the town. Only in the evenings did Ward, pleading engagements of his own, withdraw and leave Philippa and Dudley alone together.

It was a matter which, against any other background, would have provided scandalmongers with a daily feast. But the residents of the Ridge, who during the past weeks had seen nothing unusual in the close companionship of Philippa and Ward, now accepted with little comment the addition of Dudley Errol. What criticism there was came from the town. There were those who watched the three cynically; two had been company, but three? It was not easy to dislike Dudley, but he was regarded by some as a fool to risk losing his fiancée, and by others as a man too sure of himself, a man unaware of the odds against him.

Dudley's feelings, under his calm exterior, were a blend of surprise, fear and perplexity. He had not cared to admit to himself, much less to Philippa, that it was jealousy of Ward Rowallen that had brought him here before he was expected. The letters that had reached him had made him build up a picture of an interloper, a treacherous element in the guise of old family friend. But jealous as he had been on his arrival, he could find nothing in the demeanour of either Philippa or Ward to give him cause for suspicion or anxiety. The two were friendly, natural—and as far as even his anxious eyes could see, no more. Even his feeling that Ward was a dangerously attractive man could not convince him that he was a rival. The daily meetings, the busy schedule, the changes taking place on the Ridge, made for him a scene of semi-rural English life, and gradually his mind grew quiet and he ceased to probe beneath the surface. He was helped in this by Mrs. Lyle, whose placid preparations for Philippa's departure, and references to her future life with Dudley, were perhaps the most reassuring element in the situation.

Whatever the comments, whatever the gossip, it was clear that Dudley soon became universally liked. His good looks, his splendid figure, his quiet, almost grave manner, his interest in anything and everything that concerned Montoak, all these recommended him to Ridge dwellers and town dwellers alike. It was obvious that he was enjoying his visit. And Philippa's mother, who had expected that with his arrival, the neighbours would appear less often at the house, found the drawing room invaded by the MacRoberts, the Armitages, the Plesseys and even by the rubicund Mr. Springer, who seldom cared to leave his comfortable armchair in between attendances at his son's football matches.

"Nice chap," he commented, watching Philippa and Dudley driving away to have dinner in town. "She's lucky to get him, and he's lucky to get her. I hope they have a splendid pack of kids."

But the place in which Dudley liked to spend most of his time was the Manor. The lovely, neglected old house, the shady walks, the varied views of the countryside, the large, echoing, half empty rooms, seemed to fascinate him, and he never tired of walking up the hill with Philippa and joining Ward inside the Manor or around the grounds.

"It hasn't got much history," Ward explained to him. "It's just one of those old manors that should have been taken care of, but which required more money than the owner possessed."

"There must have been money once," Dudley commented.

"Long, long ago," Ward said. "The family were never good managers, and they suffered from *folie de grandeur*. Their assets never kept pace with the *folie*. The last asset vanished in about the year 1880."

"What happened in the year 1880?" Dudley enquired.

"The ninth baronet's wife ran away." Philippa spoke from the window against which she was leaning. "Let's take him to the picture gallery," she suggested, "and show him the cast."

They walked into the gallery. Dudley had seen the portraits before, but this time they led him to the imposing likeness of the ninth baronet, splendid in long, curling side whiskers and bearded chin, with his hair parted in the centre from front to back, and flattened on the forehead. On a thronelike chair beside him was placed his top hat, with tapered top and curling brim. Also on the chair was his velvet, fur trimmed overcoat. Dudley gazed at him in awe.

"My!" he said.

"He didn't always look like that," Ward said. "In his hunting outfit he looked far more businesslike."

"Did he have his hunting outfit on when he went after the runaways?" Philippa enquired.

"Fill me in about the runaways?" Dudley requested.

"Well, come over here and you'll see who did the running," Ward said. "Here's his second wife."

"She ran away?" Dudley asked.

"She did. And not alone, and not empty handed. She took most of what remained of the family fortunes."

"How could she do that?" Dudley asked. "Oxen carts filled with bullion?"

"No. She merely took a valuable gold belt—the only really valuable piece of property owned by the family. You can see it in the portrait.

"This belt?" Dudley went up to examine the portrait more closely.

"Solid gold chain," Ward said, "encrusted with what I would like to call fabulous jewels."

"She took that?"

"Yes. In a way she was entitled to it," Ward said. "The story goes that the ninth baronet gave it to her to tip the scales when she was trying to make up her mind between marrying him and accepting a continental reigning prince. He—the baronet—wasn't much of a catch, apart from the belt; he was pretty well on his beam ends. He was a widower, with two grown-up sons, and if you look more closely at the portrait you'll see that he was no oil painting."

"Where did she run to?" Dudley asked.

"Nobody'll ever know. She departed with a Borgia-type gentleman by the name of Carlos."

"Just skipped?"

"There was a kind of feast—the elder son was getting married. Halfway through the ceremony, the baronet happened to glance out of a window and saw his wife and Carlos down on the Ridge. He went out, alone, and was later found dead—the bridge had collapsed."

"Bridge?" enquired Dudley.

"I'll show you when we go down the hill," Ward said. "It was a wooden bridge, and it was used as a kind

179

of short cut if people wanted to cross the Ridge. It caved in and the baronet was drowned."

"And then what?"

"Well, the story rather peters out after that," Ward said regretfully. "He didn't get as far as the runaways. So they got away—and took the belt with them."

Dudley, fascinated, walked slowly from one portrait to the other.

"And never any sequel?" he asked.

"Never," said Ward. "But if you're interested, let's go down and take a look at where the bridge used to be."

They walked slowly down the hill, and Ward paused at the place where there had once been a small bridge, which could still be seen in old illustrations hanging in the town library. It was at the foot of the hill, and had once, Ward explained, spanned the trickle that had encouraged the Plessey sisters to build their Japanese garden, and which was now reappearing and filling his pond.

On the site, the slow careful excavation of a further and as yet unknown length of Roman pavement went on. It was here that Dudley often came, watching and reporting at lunchtime to Philippa and to Ward the progress of the work.

On the day that Philippa and her mother were attending the dress rehearsal of the Plesseys' end-of-term concert, Dudley wandered into the bar of the ancient comfortable Oak and Apple to find Ward easing himself on to a stool.

"I've ordered beer and cold chops," he told Dudley. "How about you?"

"Is it your treat, or mine?"

"Yours."

"Then beer, and a large supply of ham and beef sandwiches. I'm hungry."

180

"What have you been doing all morning?" Ward asked.

"Looking at skeletons."

Ward said nothing until the orders had come sliding down the bar towards them, and he had lowered the level of his beer to half glass. Then: "Dinosaurs?" he asked.

"No. Human."

"Really? Who?"

"They don't know, and as far as I can tell they don't much care. Their object is to get down to that pavement, and what they unearth on the way will be someone else's department."

Ward frowned thoughtfully.

"I don't remember any battles in the history of Montoak," he said, "but . . . "

"No battles. Just two people. Young, one expert said. One male, one female."

Ward's interest quickened.

"A pair? Could it have been a case of what we call dirty work at the crossroads?"

"Maybe." Dudley finished a sandwich and began on another. "It was dirty work, for sure. A bullet hole in the back of each skull, almost in the same spot—dead centre. Good shooting."

"Well, go on," urged Ward.

"Not me, brother. You've got to do the going on."

"Why me? I wasn't there when they unearthed the skeletons."

"No, you weren't. But you've got a good headpiece, with no bullet hole in it, so you could use it to think with."

His tone made Ward, who was about to embark on a second beer, put his glass down untouched.

"I don't get it," he said slowly.

"You will if you think some more. Maybe I'm on the

181

wrong track—but somehow I don't think so. The one who's been on the wrong track, it seems to me, is you. You and your forebears. You could . . . "

"Wait a minute," broke in Ward. "Are you suggesting that these two . . . "

"Well, go on. Keep at it."

"You think they might be . . . "

"You'd make a lousy detective. When I said you'd been on the wrong track, what I meant was that you assumed your ancestor was chasing the lady and her lover when he fell off the bridge. My theory is that he was on his way back home."

"Back home?" echoed Ward.

"He saw them from a window. He hadn't far to go to catch them up. He put a bullet in the back of their heads, and then he buried them—not deep, as they discovered today."

"Why bury them?"

"To hide the evidence."

"But there wouldn't have been a charge of murder. It was . . . "

"I know. *Crime passionel,* as the French say. They took a valuable belt with them, right? My bet is that he didn't bury that. He took that home with him—but he didn't get home. He got as far as the bridge. Had Sherlock Holmes been invented?"

"No," Ward said after consideration. "I think he came in the 1890s."

"Which was why the affair was so mishandled. Nobody followed the old man's tracks with a magnifying glass. Nobody put on a deerstalker cap and examined the stream. They simply buried him and assumed that the lovers were spending the proceeds of the belt in some luxurious spa on the continent. And now you've got the bodies, but that's all you've got."

They sat for a time in silence. The lunch hour was over, the bar was empty.

"If you'd like the advice of a friend"—Dudley finished his beer and sandwiches and prepared to return to the site—"it's this: keep the clues under your hat. Murder or not, this isn't the kind of family history you want to spread around the neighbourhood. Do you want to come with me and see the bodies?"

"No."

Ward watched the doors swing behind him and stood moodily staring at them for some moments. Then he walked to the Manor and went into the picture gallery. Standing in front of the portrait of the runaway wife, he stared long and intently at the belt round her waist, seeking to assess what value it would have in present day terms. A lot of gold, he mused. A thick band of gold, four inches wide and—how many?—possibly almost four feet in length. Five or six figures worth of gold. And the jewels . . . A tidy capital. Lost. The stream had drained away many years ago, leaving nothing but a stony bed. Had the belt been found? Who knew? Who would ever know?

"They're taking a long time to find the you-know-what, aren't they?" Laura asked.

"What does time matter?" Selma asked in her turn. "The thing is where it belongs. Sooner or later, someone will find it."

"I'd rather it were sooner. Then we could, as it were, share the pleasure."

"That's a selfish view, Laura."

"I suppose it is. But after going to so much trouble . . . and suppose it gets stolen?"

"What thief would decide to dig under an oak tree in case something valuable was hidden there?"

Laura had no answer to this, but she had not long to

wait for her share of the pleasure. Two days later, Chester's eldest grandchild, playing with his brother in the Manor grounds, hid, like King Charles the Second, up an oak tree. Unlike the king, he fell out of it and landed on ground recently disturbed by the treetoppers. His roars brought his grandfather hastening to the spot. After assuring himself that there was more woe than wound, he lifted the boy into his arms—and saw something on the ground that made him almost drop him again.

Ten minutes later, scouts were being sent round the town to find Ward.

They knew where to look for him. This was the day of the Plesseys' end-of-term play, and in the spacious darkened Pilgrims' Hall sat three hundred enthralled spectators, many of them clutching damp handkerchiefs. For this was a drama whose impact was the greater by reason of the extraordinary ability of the sisters to instil a theatrical tradition into their pupils. On the stage stood the infamous Roman tyrant Gallus (in private life Willie Bond, aged six) flanked by two murderous henchmen. Facing them was the diminutive, flaxen haired Calpurnia (Maureen McPhee, rising seven) and her brother, Augustus (Oliver Outhwaite, six), fearless Christians prepared to suffer martyrdom at the hands of pagan Gallus. Rome had lost its pre-eminence; Constantinople was officially Christian, but in Rome lions were still being given Christians to eat, and it seemed likely at this point of the drama that Augustus was to be next on the menu. Christians versus pagans. Virtue versus villainy. The threats of Gallus met by unflinching Christian courage.

The performers, young as they were, attired in togas or draperies improvised from Plessey sheets, held their audience like veteran actors. Ward, clutching the prompt book, had found the cast word perfect, and had allowed his interest to stray to the unfolding of the drama. So absorbing did he find this that the scouts sent out by Chester, fighting their way with difficulty through the Romans and Christians waiting in the wings, found it at first impossible to gain his attention. In the dead silence that reigned, broken only by the clear young voices on the stage, it was impossible to hiss at him. Taps on his shoulder produced only impatient shrugs and a mute order to go away and leave the way clear for the exit of Calpurnia. Not until the curtain had dropped, leaving Augustus's fate still undecided, could the scouts whisper their urgent summons.

"Chester? Go back and tell him I'm busy. I've got a job here, as you can see," Ward informed them.

"He said you had to come at once."

"He'd forgotten the play was on."

"No, he hadn't. Something's come up—something very important. He's waiting for you."

Ward frowned impatiently.

"Where is he?"

"Under an oak tree in the Manor drive."

"You mean he's hurt?"

"No, no, no. He's all right, but he won't let anybody go near him. He's waiting for you. He's kind of excited. He says nothing will get him to move until you get there."

This account was disturbing enough to cause Ward to assign his prompter's role to Gallus' father and follow the scouts out of the hall.

When he arrived at the oak tree, Chester was standing guard.

*   *   *

There was general rejoicing when the news spread. How the belt came to be buried there, nobody knew, but everybody was free to guess. Only Dudley had questions, and to those nobody could give any answers.

185

"Why look for snags?" Ward demanded. "Aren't you glad I'm going to be rich after all these years?"

"I'd just like to work the thing out, that's all," Dudley said. "It doesn't add up."

"Yes, it does," Ward contradicted. "The assessors are doing the addition at this moment. I'm in the money."

"Congratulations," said Dudley.

"And d'you know what I'm going to do with my new-found riches?" Ward went on.

"Yes. Get to work restoring the Manor."

"Right. But that's only part of it. When the restoration has been completed, it'll have a new name. The . . . " He stopped and began again. "You've learned a good deal about this town since you came to it, but there's one thing about it that you don't know, because you haven't been in a position to find out. You've spent your sojourn with the Lyles. If you'd come as a stranger, you would have had a choice of so-called inns, or a hotel which in spite of efforts on my part to improve it, has remained what it was when it first opened in the eighteen-eighties. So . . . "

"You're going into the hotel business? You mean you'll turn the Manor into . . . "

"Precisely. I've never had a real job, but this will be one after my own heart. The Manor Hotel. Owner, me. Manager, me. Staff? Well, I've got friends. I'll send you my first brochure and you can show it to your associates and tell them that this is a peaceful corner of England with a first class hotel. You see before you a future hotelier."

"Congratulations," said Dudley again.

11

The car Dudley had hired during his stay was in position outside the garage, facing the gate, the brakes holding it on the slope from the house to the road. Dudley's suitcases were already in the capacious luggage compartment. Two of Philippa's were to come, but Dudley had only a small handgrip to finish packing.

Ward had come in to say goodbye. He had some small but useful details to impart regarding the state of the road after the recent heavy rain. This said, everybody tried to find something more to say. At last Ward came out of an absorbed silence.

"Well, all the best," he said to Dudley, in a tone that sounded unfamiliar. "Come back soon." They shook hands and he turned to Philippa. "See me to the gate," he suggested. He raised a hand to Mrs. Lyle. "I'll drop by tomorrow and try to cheer you up."

He followed Philippa through the hall and out on to the road. Dudley looked after them and spoke sympathetically to Mrs. Lyle.

"She's going to feel it," he said. "I didn't think it was going to be this hard."

Mrs. Lyle found nothing to say in reply. She was very pale. Her eyes, seen in the low light of the hall, had a mournful look. As she went up the stairs, he wished passionately that he and Philippa were on their way, partings over, a new life beginning.

He picked up some small parcels and went towards the door.

"I'll put these in while I'm about it. Something tells

me we're going to be charged a whole lot of over-weight."

He entered the garage by the communicating door, at last cleared of debris by Philippa. The light was out. As he groped for the switch in the blackness, Ward's voice came clearly from the gate.

"I don't think Dudley'd mind if I kiss you goodbye. Do you?"

"I don't know." There was a tremor in Philippa's voice. "We said goodbye before he came."

"You did. If you remember, I said I wasn't going to check out until I had to—until you told me to. It's a pity he's such a nice fellow—it made things impossible from my point of view. It ought to be easier to give you up to a man like him—but somehow it isn't. I hope—oh, dearest, dearest Philippa—I hope you'll be happy. I know you'll make him happy, and I'm glad—he deserves it. All I remember is that you once came near to admitting that you loved me. I'll hang on to that."

Dudley tried to move and found it impossible. His feet seemed fixed to the concrete floor. He could see, silhouetted, the two figures. He saw Ward draw her close; he saw her faint resistance and heard her sigh as she surrendered herself to his embrace.

"That's all. I love you for ever. Bless you, my darling. The chaplain at my prep school had a poem printed to give all his confirmation candidates. I've forgotten most of it, but it began:

God bless you. If I knew some better thing to wish you
It were yours a hundredfold.

I don't know any better thing. Goodbye."

Dudley stood, still frozen, as she returned to the house. Turning, he could see her leaning against the dark windows of the drawing room, staring out as though it were still possible to see the tall form striding towards the Manor.

When he went into the room, she did not turn. He stood beside her for a time, and then took her gently by the shoulders and made her face him.

"Sad?" he asked.

"Yes. Silly, isn't it? I ought to be thinking of what I'm going to, instead of what I'm leaving. I'm sorry, Dudley—just give me time."

He put a finger on the tear that lay on her cheek.

"I love you," he said softly.

"I know. I'm so grateful for everything . . ."

"I'm the one who's got cause for gratitude." He led her to the door. "Go up to bed and sleep. You'll feel different in the morning."

She went slowly up the stairs. She did not go into her mother's room—she stood at her own window staring out into the dark, gazing up at the hill on which stood the beautiful old house, dreaming of its owner.

Left alone, Dudley finished his packing and then sat down to write a letter. His movements were slow and deliberate, and gave no hint of the tumult that was in his mind. It seemed to him that he felt every emotion but surprise. It was what he had feared. Perhaps, he admitted to himself, it was what he had known. The threat had always been there. His coming had been the result of fears and suspicions which he should not have allowed to be lulled. He had come to England to find out where Ward Rowallen fitted in—but he had come too late.

Loyalty? Something told him that it was more than loyalty that had enabled her to keep to her bargain. She loved Ward—but she had enough feeling for himself to go with him to Canada. She loved him as she had loved him when they became engaged. She loved him enough to marry him. But he knew, with complete certainty, that she would never be really happy with him. Her roots here were too deep.

The letter he wrote was not many pages long. He wrote swiftly and unhesitatingly. He put the pages into an envelope and addressed it with one word: Philippa. He went noiselessly up the stairs, put the letter against a small Dresden china figurine on a table, and placed the table outside Philippa's door so that it would be the first thing she saw on emerging. Then he went downstairs and let himself out of the house. He got into the car, released the brake and coasted down the road to the Springers' corner. Only then did he start the engine and, accelerating until his speed matched the beat of his heart, drove northward, westward, back the way he had come, back to his own land, his own life, his empty home.